"Out!" Bolan snapped

Sergeant Granger bailed out on the passenger's side. Bolan crouched behind his open driver's door and Granger found cover between two semitrailers.

Any second now...

The chase car roared into view, headlights lancing toward the parked RAV4. They had to see it, but the black car sitting there, stopped dead, would confuse them long enough for Bolan to begin the fight on his own terms. A slim advantage, but he would take what he could get.

Which, at the moment, was a clean shot through the Yukon's tinted windshield. Bolan didn't count on hitting anyone with that first round, but it forced the larger SUV to swerve away, tires screeching on the asphalt.

Breaking from his own partial concealment, Bolan sprinted in pursuit of the Yukon. He was the hunter now, whether the Yukon's occupants knew it or not. The game had turned around on them, but there was no change in the stakes.

Still life or death.

MACK BOLAN ®
The Executioner

The Executioner
Don Pendleton's ®

PATRIOT STRIKE

A GOLD EAGLE BOOK FROM
WORLDWIDE ®

TORONTO • NEW YORK • LONDON
AMSTERDAM • PARIS • SYDNEY • HAMBURG
STOCKHOLM • ATHENS • TOKYO • MILAN
MADRID • WARSAW • BUDAPEST • AUCKLAND

For Sergeant Dakota Meyer, U.S. Marine Corps

Recycling programs
for this product may
not exist in your area.

First edition April 2014

ISBN-13: 978-0-373-64425-4

Special thanks and acknowledgment to
Mike Newton for his contribution to this work.

PATRIOT STRIKE

At least two thirds of our miseries spring from human stupidity, human malice, and those great motivators and justifiers of malice and stupidity, idealism, dogmatism and proselytizing zeal on behalf of religious or political idols.

—Aldous Huxley,
*Tomorrow and Tomorrow
and Tomorrow* (1956)

We fought one civil war for the Union already. I'm shutting down the second one.

—Mack Bolan

THE
MACK BOLAN
LEGEND

Nothing less than a war could have fashioned the destiny of the man called Mack Bolan. Bolan earned the Executioner title in the jungle hell of Vietnam.

But this soldier also wore another name—Sergeant Mercy. He was so tagged because of the compassion he showed to wounded comrades-in-arms and Vietnamese civilians.

Mack Bolan's second tour of duty ended prematurely when he was given emergency leave to return home and bury his family, victims of the Mob. Then he declared a one-man war against the Mafia.

He confronted the Families head-on from coast to coast, and soon a hope of victory began to appear. But Bolan had broken society's every rule. That same society started gunning for this elusive warrior—to no avail.

So Bolan was offered amnesty to work within the system against terrorism. This time, as an employee of Uncle Sam, Bolan became Colonel John Phoenix. With a command center at Stony Man Farm in Virginia, he and his new allies—Able Team and Phoenix Force—waged relentless war on a new adversary: the KGB.

But when his one true love, April Rose, died at the hands of the Soviet terror machine, Bolan severed all ties with Establishment authority.

Now, after a lengthy lone-wolf struggle and much soul-searching, the Executioner has agreed to enter an "arm's-length" alliance with his government once more, reserving the right to pursue personal missions in his Everlasting War.

Prologue

Lubbock, Texas

The Golden Sage Motel stood on Highway 82 west of town. Also known as the Marsha Sharp Freeway—named for the former coach of Texas Tech's Lady Raiders basketball team—the highway is Lubbock's primary east-west access road, providing greater access to the university and downtown Lubbock.

But no one would ever know it from the Golden Sage.

Built when the freeway was still just plain-old Highway 82, the motel squats beside six lanes of asphalt, blank-eyed windows watching traffic pass. A few cars stop, inevitably, but a glance at fading paint, cracked cinder blocks and spotty neon signage on the fake saguaro cactus out in front quickly reveals that business isn't thriving.

Jerod Granger didn't care.

He'd checked in looking for a place to hide, taking a room around in back where passing drivers couldn't see his six-year-old Toyota Camry XV30 sitting by itself. He'd told the clerk he couldn't sleep with too much highway noise outside his window and accommodating his desire was easy, since the Golden Sage had only two guests registered when Jerod had arrived.

Three bodies for two dozen rooms. So much for economic stimulus.

He had one night to kill before tomorrow's meeting, couldn't push it forward any further. He'd said the deal was urgent, but he'd balked at saying *life or death*. That part would have to be explained in person, face-to-face, tomorrow morning.

Lubbock's FBI office, on Texas Avenue, watched over nineteen of the state's 254 counties. Lubbock, in turn, was supervised from Dallas, one of the bureau's fifty-six regional field offices scattered nationwide. Granger didn't trust the Dallas office and in fact had been advised to seek out only one of Lubbock's resident agents.

Hence the delay.

If he could trust just anyone, he could have strolled in off the street last week, sat down and told his story to the first G-man or G-woman available. That wouldn't fly, however. Not with the explosive secret he was carrying, the stakes that he was playing for. He'd asked the only person that he really trusted for some advice and had received a single name.

Case closed.

Now all he had to do was make it through the next—what? Thirteen hours and change?—to have that talk, give up his evidence and breathe a huge sigh of relief over a job well done.

A job he'd never wanted, obviously, but it made no difference. Sometimes a circumstance reached out and grabbed a guy by the throat, and wouldn't let him go.

So here he sat, on his bed in Room 19, watching a crazy show about a woman with six personalities, while he ate his KFC meal with a Ruger Super Redhawk .44 Magnum revolver beside him. It was the "small" model, with a 7.5-inch barrel versus the maximum 9.5-inch, still bigger and badder than *Dirty Harry*'s Smith & Wesson Model 29. It would kill anything that walked on two or four legs.

And Granger hoped it would keep him alive.

By this time tomorrow he would be in protective custody—assuming he lived that long and that any such thing still existed. Granger wasn't even sure the FBI *could* protect him.

Still it was the best chance he had left. His only chance.

The wacky chick on TV was dressed like a man now, drinking a longneck Corona and scratching herself like a truck driver in a strip club. Hell, she *was* in a strip club, paying ten bucks for a lap dance. Granger scowled and switched it off with the remote, not minding nudity but put off by what he regarded as the program's sheer absurdity. He reached out for his soda can, ready to wash down some of the colonel's original recipe—and found it empty.

"Crap!"

The pop machine was four doors down from Granger's room, tucked into an alcove with an ice machine at the motel's northeast corner. He didn't like going outside in the dark, not tonight, but the chicken was stuck in his throat now. There went another dollar fifty for a can of fizzing syrup that he used to get for half a buck.

He took the Ruger, tucked it inside the waistband of his slacks as best he could and donned a jacket to conceal it. Desert nights were cold, so no one would think twice about the jacket, and he didn't plan on meeting anybody, anyway. He was the only tenant on the backside of the Golden Sage, nothing but open land and scrub brush stretching away into the night.

Granger made sure to take his key, the beige door locking automatically behind him. No surprises waiting for him when he came back with his overpriced drink in its plastic ice bucket. A short walk, out and back. No problem.

Until the black Cadillac Escalade rolled into view, its high beams nearly blinding him.

Granger didn't react at first, telling himself it might just be another guest arriving, then his brain kicked into gear, asking him why in hell the owner of a brand-new Escalade would spend five minutes at the Golden Sage Motel.

No reason in the world, unless he happened to be hunting.

As the Caddy's doors swung open, Granger dropped his empty bucket and started hauling on the Ruger. Snagged its front sight on his Jockey shorts but ripped it free, aiming the big wheel gun with trembling hands. He noted four men flat-footed by the Escalade, its driver still behind the wheel, and fired once at the nearest of them, praying for a hit. It felt miraculous, seeing the big man topple over backward, going down.

Granger was running then, with gunfire snapping, crackling and popping in the night behind him. He ran past his room and kept on going past his Camry, since the keys were in the motel and there was no time to get in the car anyway. Running like his life depended on it.

Which, of course, it did.

The first rounds struck him when he'd covered all of twenty yards. They lifted Jerod Granger and propelled him forward, airborne, arms and legs windmilling as he found that he could fly. It was a freaking miracle.

But landing was a bitch.

The sidewalk rushed to meet him, struck the left side of his face with force enough to crack the cheekbone. Granger scarcely felt it, going numb already. He could barely find the strength to feel for his Ruger, but the gun had slipped beyond his reach.

Like life itself.

Footsteps approached him, voices muttering as if from miles away and underwater. By the time his killers started firing down into Jerod's back and skull, he was already gone.

1

San Antonio, Texas

Midnight at the Alamo. Not dark—spotlights shone off the old mission's facade—but, hanging back a hundred yards, Mack Bolan, aka the Executioner, still found shadows to conceal him as he walked a circuit of the battle site.

Once upon a troubled time, the Alamo had stood on San Antonio's eastern outskirts. Today it commands a plaza downtown, surrounded by streets named for marytrs: Bonham, Bowie, Crockett, Travis. Men who had stood their ground and had died for an idea called Texas.

Bolan's first impression of the place was mild disappointment. He had expected more, somehow, from a national shrine. Something *larger,* perhaps, than the squat adobe-brick structure before him. Sixty-three feet wide and twenty-three feet tall, besides the parapet, extending back one-hundred-odd feet from the plaza in front.

Not much to it, until factoring in 189 defenders, mostly civilians, fighting to the death against some eighteen hundred trained regulars, both infantry and cavalry.

Remember the Alamo? San Antonians don't have much choice.

Bolan wasn't here to study history or pay his personal respect to heroes, though he did that automatically, at any battleground or military graveyard. He was at the Alamo to keep a date, obtain some information, maybe save some lives.

How many? That was still an open question, which he hoped to answer as soon as he spoke to his contact.

A Texas Ranger, no less. How perfect was that?

Bolan had flown into San Antonio International Airport from Dulles, in Virginia, and then rented a silver Toyota RAV4. His ID—a more-or-less genuine Texas driver's license in the name of Matthew Cooper—had served him well at his previous stop, a store with broad, barred windows whose tall neon sign promised Guns! Guns! Guns!

Thanks to Texas's lax firearms legislation, Bolan's purchases included an AR-15 rifle, the civilian semi-auto version of an M16A1; a Benelli M4 Super 90 semi-auto twelve-gauge shotgun with extended magazine and collapsible buttstock; a matched pair of Glock 22 pistols, chambered in .40 S&W; and a Buckmaster 184 survival knife. He added a fast-draw shoulder rig, a clip-on holster for his belt, two dozen extra magazines and all the ammo he could carry. Bolan paid cash—lifted from an L.A. crack dealer some months before—and made the salesman's day.

"Y'all come back now, hear?"

A little tinkering would turn the AR-15 into a full-auto weapon if Bolan had the time. Meanwhile it was a good killing machine straight off the rack. He would have liked at least one sound suppressor for the Glocks, but that meant filling out a lot of Class III paperwork and waiting while it cycled through the ATF labyrinth in Washington. In a pinch, the Buckmaster was quieter than any firearm and never had to be reloaded. He'd simply have to be up close and personal when he went in for the kill.

This was supposed to be a peaceful meeting, though. No fuss, no muss, no bodies on the ground.

Supposed to be.

So here at the Alamo, he wore the Glocks and knife concealed, leaving the rifle and the shotgun in his rented SUV. He had parked it down on Crockett Street and had walked back to the Alamo, dodging the streetlights where he could. If all went well, it was a relatively short walk back to catch his ride. If not, two blocks could be a lethal gauntlet.

Fifteen rounds in each Glock's magazine, plus two spares in the pouches on his shoulder rig and two more in his pockets. Enough to stop a midsized company of soldiers, but it only took one lucky shot by an opponent and the game was over. Bolan could die and never know what hit him, sure. The way a combat soldier always hoped to go, if old age wasn't on the table.

But until that happened, he was working every angle for security. Taking nothing for granted beyond his next step, his next breath.

"WHERE IS SHE?" Jesse Folsom muttered.

"Runnin' late," Bryar Haskin said. "How the hell should I know?"

"We just sit and wait for her?" asked Jimmy Don Bodine.

"Naw," Haskin answered back. "We gonna go 'n' get a lap dance, then tell Kent we didn't wanna stick around. How's that sound to ya? Think he'll like it?"

"I just meant—"

"Check this out," Cletus Jackson said, from the backseat.

A car was turning north from Crockett onto Alamo Plaza. It slowed for the parking lot's entrance, then swung in it. Creeping along, the vehicle slid into a space about two hundred feet from the old Mexican mission.

"That her?" Folsom prodded.

"Can't tell," Jackson said. "Wait and see, with the dome light."

The car was a black Dodge Avenger, four door, not an obvious cop car. Haskin puzzled over that, since they were waiting for a cop—a *lady* cop, at that—but he supposed that she could be off duty, driving her own vehicle. It didn't matter what she came in, after all, as long as she went home with them.

The cop…and whoever she was meeting at the Alamo.

"I still can't see the driver," Jackson said, to no one in particular.

"It's one of 'em," said Haskin. "Has to be. Who else would be here when the place is closed?"

"Damn tourists," Bodine suggested. "Wanna snap a picture standin' in the lights."

"Parkin' as far as they can get from anything?" Haskin snorted dismissively. "We got one. Now just keep your eyes peeled for the other."

"You figure they'll be packin'?" Jackson asked him.

"Wouldn't you be?"

"Hell, I *am*."

That was a fact. Between them, they were carrying two pump-action shotguns, one Heckler & Koch HK416 carbine chambered in 5.56 NATO, one AK-101 feeding the same NATO rounds and at least four handguns. Bodine sometimes wore a second pistol in an ankle holster for backup, normally a Colt .380 Mustang Pocketlite, but Haskin hadn't looked to see if he was packing it tonight.

They had firepower, anyhow, and horsepower under the hood of their GMC Yukon, with its 5.7-liter turbocharged Chevrolet small-block V8 engine. Haskin wished they'd had a bit more *brain*power, but these were good boys, dedicated, all straight shooters. He would work with what he had.

And how hard could it be?

Pick up two people from the ever-loving Shrine of Texas Liberty and take them back to headquarters for questioning. It wasn't like they had to fight John Wayne and Richard Widmark, or even Billy Bob Thornton. Sure, one of them was a Texas Ranger, but she was a *woman,* for God's sake.

One woman then and she'd be packing, but he didn't know about the other one. Haskin had no idea who else they were looking for—a man or woman; white, black or whatever—but it stood to reason that there'd be at least one other gun against their eight or nine.

Safe odds, if only they had been allowed to kill their quarry, but that wasn't in the cards. His orders were to bring at least one of them back alive and preferably both. Headquarters couldn't question corpses, and if Haskin dropped the ball on this one, it would be his own ass on the charcoal grill. And that was not one of them whatchamacallits. Simile or metaphor, maybe an oxymoron.

Screw it.

"Here goes," said Jackson, as the Dodge Avenger's driver opened up her door and stepped out. She'd turned the dome light off—smart thinking—but the parking lot was lit for security's sake, and Haskin recognized her from a photo he'd been shown that afternoon.

"It's her," he said. The lady Ranger.

"One down, one to go," said Bodine, like he had just invented math.

"Suppose the other one don't show?" asked Folsom.

"Then we bag this one," Haskin replied. "Call it a night."

"We have to take her straight back?" Jackson queried. "She's a looker."

"Remember what we're here for, damn it. And remember what you stand to lose, if you screw it up."

WATCHING FROM THE SHADOWS, Bolan saw his contact step out of a vehicle he took to be her personal ride. Nothing the Texas Rangers would select for chasing outlaws on the open road, and Bolan wasn't sure if they did any undercover work. He knew the force was small—about 150 officers to police America's second-largest state and its twenty-six million inhabitants. Not to mention the countless tourists, drifters and undocumented aliens. Only a handful of Rangers were women, and Bolan was looking at one of them now.

He knew her face from photos he'd received in preparation for the meeting. She, on the other hand, wouldn't know him from Adam until Bolan introduced himself. Photos of Bolan—with the new face he had worn since "dying" some time back in New York City's Central Park—were scarce as the proverbial hen's teeth. He hadn't bothered changing fingerprints at the same time, since he was dead to the world, and Uncle Sam's elves had purged every file they could find that contained Bolan's prints—from the Pentagon and FBI headquarters, to LAPD, NYPD and so on down the food chain.

In that sense, at least, it was good to be dead.

The Ranger he had come to meet, by contrast, was very much alive. And Bolan hoped to help her stay that way.

Adlene Granger was thirty-one years old, five-seven without standard Ranger cowboy boots and Stetson hat, her frame packed with 137 fairly trim, athletic pounds. Green eyes and auburn hair, no known tattoos, although she had a scar inside her left forearm from taking down a crackhead who had pulled a razor in the scuffle. All of that was in her file, together with the fact that she had shot two would-be bank robbers in Brownsville, on a stakeout, killing one of them.

But now she needed help and couldn't ask her fellow Rangers. Couldn't put her faith in local law enforcement, Texas-style. She wasn't all that keen on trusting Feds—from what Bolan understood—but everybody had to lean on someone, sometime.

Nature's law.

Enter the Executioner.

His contact—Ranger Granger?—had a tale to tell, and Bolan had agreed to listen. He already knew the basics from his briefing, but he needed more details. Needed to know if it was serious enough to rate his kind of handling and yield a positive result.

Bolan had known too many dedicated and courageous women of the law to swallow any crap about their runaway emotions, inability to cope with crises or the rest of it. Short of a power-lifting contest in the heavyweight division, Bolan couldn't think of any field where women did not rival or surpass their male competitors—and he had seen some Russian ladies who could hoist the big iron, too.

He wasn't looking for a partner, though. Had no intention of enlisting anybody for his mission, if it turned out that there *was* a mission here, deep in the heart of Texas. He wanted information he could act on—if it seemed his kind of action was appropriate—while Ranger Granger went back to her normal daily life and put their meeting out of mind as best she could.

Simple—unless it wasn't.

Bolan knew she had a personal connection to the problem, but he didn't know how far she planned to chase it. He would have to make it crystal clear that he was not recruiting, not inviting her to join in a crusade. She would be briefing him and nothing more.

He hoped.

Emerging from the shadows, Bolan showed himself, waited and watched her start the long walk from her Dodge Avenger toward the south end of the Alamo's facade. She took long, determined strides, an easy swing to her arms. She wore handtooled boots with sharply pointed toes, blue jeans, a denim shirt under a thigh-length suede jacket. The jacket was unbuttoned, granting easy access to a good-sized pistol on her right hip, worn in a high-rise holster.

Here we go, he thought, standing his ground.

"You see 'im?" Jackson blurted out.

"We ain't blind," Haskin told him.

"Let's get after 'em," said Bodine.

"Not yet."

"Why the hell not?" Folsom challenged.

"Look, we know it's her and *likely* him, but I ain't making no mistakes 'cause we got hasty."

"What, you think he's just some random guy walkin' around the Alamo?" asked Jackson.

"Making sure don't cost us nothin' but a little time. And they ain't goin' nowhere."

"Oh, yeah? Suppose his wheels is back there and they just take off?"

"We ain't afoot," Haskin reminded him. "And Kent didn't put you in charge."

"Hey, I'm just sayin'—"

"Shut your piehole, will ya? Lemme see what's goin' on."

"Yeah, yeah."

At times like this, Bryar Haskin wished he didn't have to deal with idiots. They were useful, in their way, but Christ, their whining grated on his nerves.

He watched the woman walk toward the man who had appeared as if from nowhere—meaning that he'd walked up somewhere from the south, maybe approached by way of Crockett Street. Whatever. He was here now, if it *was* him, and while Haskin had no serious concerns on that score, he was still determined to be sure before he made a move.

It was interesting that the guy, whoever he was, made no attempt to meet the woman halfway. He hung close to the Alamo, ready to duck back out of sight and under cover at the first suggestion of a trap. A cagey bastard and corralling him could take some doing. Granted, Haskin had three men to back him, odds of two-to-one, but if the man and woman separated, and it turned into a foot chase, they were screwed. He didn't plan to run around the Alamo all night, like some dumb cluck in one of *The Three Stooges* comedies.

And what if someone started shooting? They'd have cops up the wazoo in nothing flat, the very last thing he needed on a job like this. He thought about the shit storm that would rain down on him if he got arrested, and it made his chili supper curdle in his stomach.

Not a freakin' chance.

Haskin clutched his Ithaca 37 shotgun—the Deerslayer Police Special version—in hands that were suddenly sweaty. At first he had relished being in charge of this mission, taking it as a sign of advancement, but now he saw how it could blow up in his face. Spoil everything, in fact. And it would be his fault if anything went wrong.

Across the parking lot, the lady Ranger was within twenty feet of Mr. X and closing in. They hadn't started talking yet, as far as Haskin could tell, but he couldn't swear to it. There'd likely be some kind of recognition signal, or a password, then they'd either start to do their business or the Ranger would bail out, if she discovered the guy wasn't who she had come to meet.

The odds of that were nil, but Haskin wasn't taking any chances.

Wait and see.

Now they were close enough to speak without raising their voices, and he wished he'd brought a shotgun microphone to supplement the Ithaca. Something to let him eavesdrop for a little while before they rushed the couple, maybe pick up something useful for the chief, in case one or both of the targets went down for the count or was trained to resist interrogation. It would stand him in good stead, a little extra boost, but thinking of it now did Haskin no damned good at all.

"We goin' in or what?" Bodine asked.

"Hang on a sec," said Haskin.

"But—"

"You heard me!"

"Jeez."

He knew that it was risky, waiting, but he had to do this right the first time. There would be no do-overs. Wishing he'd brought more men or spread the ones he had around the park with walkie-talkies, Haskin scowled into the night.

"All right," he said at last. "Hit it!"

"What brings you to the Alamo at night, mister?" the Ranger asked when she was twenty feet away.

"Greetings from your uncles," Bolan told her.

"Uncles?"

"Sam and Hal."

"That makes you…?"

Knowing she had the name and nothing more, he told her, "Matthew Cooper."

"I'm Adlene Granger. *Sergeant* Granger."

"Right."

"You want to see ID?" She reached toward an inside jacket pocket.

Bolan waved it off. "Been there, done that."

"So there's a file on me?" she said, half smiling.

"There's a file on everyone."

"I wasn't sure you'd come," she said, shifting gears.

"Well, here I am."

"And you know what this is about?"

"Not all. The basics," Bolan answered. "I was told you'd fill me in."

"Right here?"

"Your call," Bolan said. "We can take a walk, a ride, whatever."

"You weren't followed?"

"No." He'd spent some forty minutes driving aimlessly through San Antonio to guarantee it.

"I guess this is as good as anyplace," she said. "But maybe we could step out of the light."

As if on cue, a set of high beams blazed to life, pinning them where they stood. Bolan made out the hulking shape of what appeared to be a full-sized SUV, charging from its hiding place behind the screen of trees surrounding Alamo Plaza. It hadn't trailed Granger's Dodge, meaning it had been in place *before* the meet, its occupants apprised of when and where to strike.

"You said—"

"They didn't follow me," Bolan assured her, as his Glock cleared armpit leather.

Adlene Granger drew her own sidearm, a Heckler & Koch HK45, and raised it in a firm two-handed grip. "I can't believe I missed them, damn it!"

"Who says you did?"

"But—"

"We should go," he told her.

"They're between us and my ride," she said.

"Not mine," he said. "Come on."

She almost seemed reluctant not to stay and fight it out, but turned and followed Bolan at a sprint, the SUV roaring across the parking lot behind them. The headlights tracked them until they cut around the rear end of the Alamo and ran into another line of trees.

"What about my car?" she called to Bolan.

"We'll come back for it," he said. Skipped the obvious, not adding, *if we can.*

A twelve-gauge blast echoed out behind them, buckshot chipping the flagstone walk that had been laid around the old mission-cum-fortress. It was hasty, not a good shot, but they couldn't count on someone with a shotgun missing them consistently.

Bolan was grateful for the cover when they reached the tree line, doubly glad that architects and landscapers hadn't designed any access to the property on this side of the Alamo. Unless the SUV was supercharged, with a bulldozer blade attached, its driver would be forced to turn around and circle north or south around the plaza to pick up their trail.

It was a lucky break, but nothing more. They still had two long blocks to cover before they reached his rental on Crockett Street. The shooters could reverse their course and gain some ground, but they'd be confined to streets, while Bolan and the Ranger could run in a straight line, due south to his ride.

"Jesus!" Adlene Granger gasped, close on his heels. "If they knew I was coming here—"

She didn't have to finish it. Prior knowledge meant a leak somewhere. It meant someone on her short list, one of the people she trusted, had no place there. Bolan, reasonably certain the tip hadn't originated from his side, wondered how far the lapse would set them back.

Or whether it would get them killed.

They made it to the RAV4. Bolan keyed the automatic locks from half a block away, hearing the chime, seeing the taillights flash once. He slid behind the wheel, let Adlene take the shotgun seat and gunned the straight-four 1AZ-FSE engine. Peeling out on Crockett, eastbound, he saw headlights racing down Alamo Plaza, then turning to follow him.

So much for shaking the tail.

"Are you ready for this?" he asked Granger.

Half turned in her seat, pistol still in her hand, she replied, "Bet your ass."

There it was then. Game time.

2

Washington, D.C.—Earlier

Mack Bolan stood before the National Law Enforcement Officers Memorial, considering its four bronze lions—two male and two female—guarding a pair of cubs. Beneath each brooding cat he found a carved inscription. Tacitus, from ancient Rome, stated *In valor there is hope.* The Book of Proverbs reminded Bolan that *The wicked flee when no man pursueth: but the righteous are as bold as a lion.*

He wasn't sure about the second part, having known some so-called righteous folks who didn't have the courage of their own convictions. He could buy the first bit, though. The wicked could run, but they couldn't hide.

At least not from the Executioner.

Bolan's visit to Washington, and to this memorial in particular, was not a matter of coincidence. He wasn't a casual tourist and most emphatically was not on vacation. He had come to meet one of his oldest living friends, a certified member of an endangered species, to discuss a matter of the utmost urgency.

Or so Bolan had been told.

This friend, Hal Brognola, had an office nearby, in the Robert F. Kennedy Department of Justice Building on Pennsylvania Avenue. Bolan had not seen it from the inside, and he likely never would. Although no longer wanted by the Feds and physically unrecognizable to those who'd hunted him during his long one-man campaign against the Cosa Nostra, Bolan knew that strolling through the halls of justice would be deemed a breach of etiquette. How could he be there, anyway, when he officially did not exist?

So, when he got an urgent call from Brognola, they either met at Stony Man—a working farm and the nerve center of the clandestine operation Bolan served, sequestered in the Blue Ridge Mountains—or at some public location in or near D.C. Crowds kept the pair of them anonymous, while they discussed their bloody business with a modicum of privacy.

Hiding in plain sight.

Today Bolan perused the names of fallen heroes who'd been shot, stabbed, bombed and bludgeoned while defending those in peril. Some had died in car crashes, during hot pursuits or when their aircraft had plummeted to earth on a surveillance mission. Others had succumbed to strokes or heart attacks on duty. Buildings had collapsed on some, as in New York on 9/11. Some had been cut down by friendly fire.

It was a war out there, as Bolan knew too well from personal experience.

He would have liked to say the good guys were winning, but each day the news refuted it.

Part of the memorial was still under construction—a National Law Enforcement Museum authorized in 2000 and scheduled to open in 2015. Bolan hoped he'd be around to visit it sometime. For now he stood and watched the workmen from a distance while a stocky figure sidled up to join him.

"Planning to pitch in?" Brognola asked.

"Not my kind of tools," Bolan replied. He was more inclined toward the demolition side of things.

"Good flight?"

"The usual."

Bolan had been in San Diego, visiting his brother, when the call from Washington had come through. A red-eye flight from San Diego International to Dulles, through Chicago O'Hare, had delivered him in time for breakfast and his meeting with Brognola.

"How's Johnny?"

"Busy," Bolan said. "What did they used to say at Pinkerton's? The eye that never sleeps?"

"Gets bloodshot," Brognola replied. "I hope he's working on a low profile."

"I think the spot as P.I. to the stars was taken."

"Just as well. If he starts showing up on the entertainment channel, it might ring somebody's bell."

"He's covered," Bolan said, hoping that it was true.

"Ready to take a walk?"

"I thought you'd never ask."

They strolled past waist-high curving granite walls decorated here and there by wreaths, bouquets and brightly colored bits of paper bearing messages of love and sorrow. To their left, a woman in her mid-thirties knelt, tracing one of the names as Bolan had seen others do at the Vietnam Veterans Memorial.

"What do you know about secession?" Hal inquired.

"It didn't work out well for the Confederacy," Bolan said.

"I mean more recently."

"I've heard some rumbles. Saw something on CNN."

"After the last election, Boston Tea Party types in all fifty states filed petitions for secession from the Union," Hal informed him. "Most of them were no more than farts in a whirlwind. You need twenty-five thousand signatures to garner a response from the White House, and most didn't come close. Texas led the field with over one hundred twenty-five thousand signatures. On the other hand, a petition to deport everyone who signed a petition to withdraw their state from the U.S. has close to thirty thousand signatures, and it's still growing."

Bolan smiled at that. "Is secession even legal?"

"Nope. Doesn't stop the nuts from trying, though."

"Not much we can do about that," Bolan said. "If I remember my high school government class, the right to petition is guaranteed by the First Amendment."

"And it's not the scribblers who concern me," said Brognola.

"I was thinking more about the flakes who just might try to pull it off."

"Anyone in particular?"

"As a matter of fact," Hal replied, "there might be."

"*Might* be?"

"Here's the deal. Three nights ago, in Lubbock, Texas, persons unknown killed a fellow named Jerod Granger. Don't worry if you've never heard of him. It barely made the news in Texas, much less anywhere outside the state."

"But you're aware of it."

"Only because I know his family. Back in the day when I was with the Bureau's field office in Dallas, my partner and I got assigned to a case in that neck of the woods. Kidnapping for ransom that turned into murder. You know the G gets in on those under the Lindbergh Law, presumption of interstate flight, yada, yada. Anyway, while we were working it, I got to know a Texas Ranger who was on the case. Lou Granger."

"Relative of the victim?"

"His father. We stayed friendly, which doesn't happen often, and we kept in touch after I transferred out of Texas. For a while there, Jerod and his sister used to call me Uncle Hal. Go figure, eh?"

"Why not?"

Hal shrugged. "Anyway, the day after Jerod went down, I got a call from his sister, Adlene. She's a Ranger now herself. Jerod had phoned her to arrange a meeting with a G-man, ultraurgent. Spoke about secession and catastrophe, gave up some names but wouldn't cover any details on the phone. Jerod had a face-to-face lined up the next morning with sis's trusted number one guy, but Jerod never made it. Next thing Adlene knows, she's making an I.D. for the Lubbock County coroner."

"And then she called you."

"Right. Not much to offer in the way of evidence, but when I got the gist of it and heard the names…well, something clicked. It's worth a closer look, I think."

"How are the parents taking it?" asked Bolan.

"Cancer took the mother, Jeannie, back in '95. Lou bought it in a single-car collision two years later."

"Rough," Bolan said.

"So, anyhow, I said I'd see what I could do. What *we* could do."

"Except she thinks that 'we' would be the Bureau?"

"Hmm."

"Why not the Rangers, since she's one of them?"

"There could be problems with security."

"The FBI? Homeland Security?"

"Both say the information is too vague, one of the names too prominent. Plus this is Texas. They're still having nightmares over Waco."

"When you say 'too prominent,' who are we looking at?" Bolan asked.

"Have you heard of L. E. Ridgway?"

"Rings a distant bell," Bolan said, "but I can't place him offhand."

"No great surprise. The 'L. E.' stands for Lamar Emerson. He's the founder, president and CEO of Lone Star Petroleum and Aerospace Technology."

"That's not a common merger, is it?"

"Not at all. In fact," Hal said, "from what I gather, it's unique. Lamar made his first couple billion from the East Texas Oil Field, pumping crude and natural gas in the fifties. Today he's got rigs all over the state and offshore. The aerospace deal fell into his lap when NASA started cutting back on some of its programs. He started out making components for their rockets and space shuttles, then got the bright idea of privatizing outer space."

"Say what?"

"You heard me right," Hal said. "Lone Star is planning junkets to the moon aboard their own space craft, beginning sometime in the next couple years. They're catering primarily to governments, with a projected round-trip price tag of one-point-five billion dollars, but private parties who can foot the bill are also welcome."

"So, if you're Bill Gates and you want to take the flight of a lifetime, they'll send you?"

"Just imagine," Hal said. "The Koch brothers can take off and *really* look down on us earthlings."

"Well, it's odd, I grant you."

"Here's the kicker. For as long as he's been filthy rich, Ridgway has been a top contributor to far-right causes. Started with the Birch Society and veered off toward the fringe from there. Militias, neo-Nazis, Klans, Army of God—"

"The clinic bombers?"

"Yep. With friends like those, you know he has to be *pro-*life. But lately he's been concentrating on a home-grown bunch of mixed nuts calling themselves the New Texas Republic."

"And we're back to secession," said Bolan.

"In spades. They started out running maneuvers, getting ready to defend us from some kind of weird *Red Dawn* scenario, plus armed patrols along the border for illegals. Now they claim the country can't be saved. It's too far gone with socialism, communism, fascism, Sharia law—they aren't exactly scholars, if you get my drift."

"And Ridgway's keeping them afloat?"

"In high style," said Brognola.

"Maybe he could send them to the moon."

"Funny you'd mention that. About those rockets…"

Bolan felt a chill, although the morning sun was warm.

"In that last call from Jerod to his sister, there was mention of fissile material."

The stuff that caused chain reactions in nuclear fission. The modern Big Bang.

"And Homeland still won't touch it?"

"Not until we have a better case," Brognola said.

"Okay. Let's hear the rest."

The rest—or most of it—was in files on a CD Brognola gave to Bolan for more leisurely perusal, while he waited for his flight to Texas. Adlene Granger was expecting him—expecting *someone*—for a meet in San Antonio at midnight. Why she'd picked the Alamo was anybody's guess. As good a choice as any, if it worked; as bad as any other, if it didn't.

At Dulles, Bolan found a corner seat near his departure gate, back to the wall, and used earbuds to keep anyone nearby from eavesdropping. The files, as usual, included still photos, video clips and facsimiles of documents.

First up was a biography of L. E. Ridgway, from his humble roots in Oklahoma through his first East Texas oil strike, the remarkable bad luck that haunted his competitors—fires and explosions, vandalism to their rigs and vehicles, some disappearances—and his advance to the top of the Fortune 500 list.

While his business and his wealth grew, the FBI began to notice his increased financing of far-right extremist groups—all dedicated to the proposition that America was under siege by enemies within; as well as standard adversaries like the Russians, North Koreans and Chinese. Ridgway and his compatriots apparently believed that every U.S. president since Herbert Hoover was a communist, a fascist or some whacky, nonsensical combination of the two.

These extremists hated government, minorities, the very concept of diversity and fumed nonstop about ephemeral conspiracies to persecute white Christian men. As for the ladies, the members thought they should just stay home, cook dinner, tend to the kids—and, if required, help clean the guns.

Not all of the yahoos were just talk, of course. Several groups that Ridgway had supported over time were linked to acts of domestic terrorism. Everybody knew about the Klan's shenanigans—cross burnings, bombings, drunken drive-by shootings.

But Ridgway had also been connected to a handful of so-called militia groups that had stockpiled illegal weapons, threatened government officials and conspired on various occasions to attack public facilities: federal buildings, natural gas pipelines—never Ridgway's—and power plants.

One "Aryan" gang wanted to poison a midsized city's water supply in Arkansas, but state police foiled their plan. None of the indictments from those cases ever touched Ridgway or Lone Star Petroleum, but Ridgway lurked in the background like a fat old spider spinning its web.

The move into privatized aerospace technology had been a break from Ridgway's normal style. He was literally going where no man had gone before, hiring personnel laid off by NASA, planning to conquer space and turn a tidy profit in the process. With billions to spend, he had acquired a decommissioned space shuttle, set his team to work improving it and pronounced it ready to soar.

Media reports claimed Lone Star Aerospace was near completion of the solid rocket boosters necessary for a launch, along with an overhauled Lunar Excursion Module—the LM-14, scrapped when plans for Apollo 19 fell through—and a snazzy Lunar Roving Vehicle. Show up with a truckload of cash and anyone could drive a dune buggy around the dark side of the moon.

There was nothing on the CD about fissile material. Bolan would have to hear that from the Ranger, assuming there was anything to tell.

From Ridgway, he moved on to Hal's files on the New Texas Republic, a secessionist militia outfit based in Tom Green County, near San Angelo, Texas. Headquarters was a rural compound squatting on scrubland west of town, home to eighty-odd families, by the FBI's estimate.

The NTR's founder and crackpot-in-chief was Waylon David Crockett, a self-proclaimed descendant of Davy Crockett, one-time Tennessee congressman and Alamo martyr. That genealogical link had never been confirmed officially, but Waylon's adherents in the NTR were satisfied.

Crockett had grown up poor and tough in Brownsville, on the Tex-Mex border. Starting at the tender age of fifteen, he had been arrested nineteen times, convicted on two juvie raps and three adult charges. The most serious, drug dealing, had sent him to Huntsville's prison for a five-year stay, but he was paroled in three.

Crockett had found the Lord while he was caged, and came out preaching a mix of politics and ultrafundamentalist religion, picking up disciples as he had roamed across the countryside. He first hooked up with Ridgway shortly after 9/11, when Crockett joined the Midland Militia, ready to defend his state against a rampaging Islamic horde that never showed up. Three years later he'd branched out on his own with the NTR and welcomed Ridgway's whole-hearted financial support.

The New Texas Republic hadn't been accused of any criminal infractions yet, but it was on watch lists maintained by the FBI, ATF and Homeland Security. Budgetary constraints and Crockett's strict screening process for new recruits had foiled any covert infiltration so far, but there were always rumors: hidden arsenals, inflammatory words, dire schemes.

Crockett's second in command was Kent Luttrell, ex-Klansman, ex-security guard for the Aryan Nations "church" compound in Idaho, ex-member of California's Minuteman Project—the "citizens' vigilance" border patrol praised by Governor Schwarzenegger in 2005 for doing "a terrific job" against illegal immigrants.

Five years running, Kent had made news for holding candlelight prayer vigils on June 11, the date when Oklahoma City bomber Timothy McVeigh was executed for mass murder. Now Kent was the NTR's sergeant-at-arms, enforcing discipline and supervising details of the minuscule "republic's" daily operations for his chief.

The two of them made a peculiar pair. Crockett was five foot five and wiry, had a Charlie Manson smile and looked like he'd forgotten how to use a comb around the time he quit high school. Most of his photos showed a face with sunken cheeks and stubble, bushy brows and dark eyes possessed of a thousand-yard stare. He wasn't quite the Unabomber, but a stranger could have been excused for thinking Crockett and Kaczynski had been separated at birth.

Luttrell, by contrast, was a strapping six foot five, clearly a bodybuilder, with a blond buzz cut and narrow brows to match. His thick arms swarmed with typical tattoos—iron crosses, lightning bolts and swastikas, the usual—while the police files said his broad back bore a life-sized portrait of *Der Führer* dressed in shining armor, battle flag unfurled.

That had to have stung.

Photos depicting Crockett and Luttrell together showed a Mutt and Jeff team—almost comical until you thought about their records and their crazed philosophy. They had been dangerous as individuals, before they met. Together, Bolan reckoned, they were even worse.

The New Texas Republic had an estimated 650 members, half of those residing more or less full-time at Crockett's Tom Green County compound. A few of the others were locked up on various charges, mostly weapons' violations or domestic violence, with the remainder at large throughout Texas. Bolan viewed the available mug shots and candid photos, memorizing the angry faces for future reference, in case they crossed his path.

Finally he turned to Adlene Granger's file. It surprised him to discover that she'd joined the U.S. Army out of high school, age eighteen, with the announced intent of making a career in uniform. The 9/11 strikes occurred when she was two years in, and she'd been posted to Afghanistan.

Two tours over there, with action around Kandahar and Tora Bora, had changed her mind about an army life, but not the uniform. She'd separated from the service at twenty-two and had joined the Texas Rangers when they had started taking on women to prove they were diverse. She'd earned her sergeant's stripes last year, something to celebrate.

Now she had lost the final member of her family to unknown gunmen. She knew he needed to report something urgent, but he wouldn't share details on the telephone. Ridgway was mentioned and the NTR, something about fissile material, but Jerod Granger had not lived to pass on anything more.

Adlene had considered talking to her boss in Austin, then decided she should try her Uncle Hal, instead.

Bolan had no idea what he would find in Texas. Maybe nothing but the paranoid delusions of a dead man—but if that were true, who'd want him dead? From the description of his body and the crime scene, it had been a more-or-less professional elimination. At the very least, Bolan knew the shooters had experience. They'd killed before and had gotten away with it.

But maybe not this time.

Bolan wasn't, strictly speaking, in the vengeance business. He wouldn't mind taking out the team that had killed Jerod Granger—three different weapons had been confirmed—but that didn't rate a call from Stony Man or a flight to San Antonio. He would assess the situation once he'd heard the Ranger's story and decide on where to go from there.

Full speed ahead or back to Washington with a report for Hal, scrubbing the job.

If Ridgway, Lone Star and the NTR were up to something wicked—*planning a catastrophe,* in Jerod Granger's words—Bolan would see the mission through. If it was all just smoke and mirrors, another zany pipe dream from the "New World Order" crowd, he'd walk away.

He heard his flight's first boarding call, erased the CD and switched off his laptop, then headed toward the gate, hoping he wouldn't have to share his row with some behemoth or an infant that would wail for fourteen hundred miles, across four states. A little peace and quiet would be nice.

But something told him that it wouldn't last for long.

3

San Antonio—Now

Rolling east on Crockett, Bolan soon found himself approaching Bowie Street. He could go north or south from there, not straight, since one-way Elm Street turned to meet him up ahead, barring access to the north-south lanes of Interstate 37.

Turning left on Bowie would propel them north to Fourth Street, back toward downtown San Antonio. A right-hand turn would lead south to Market Street, which then became South Bowie, just to keep drivers confused. South Bowie granted access to the interstate, but if Bolan stuck to surface streets, he would be leading his pursuers into residential neighborhoods.

No decent choices, either way.

Whichever way he chose, he risked having cops join the parade and putting bystanders in danger. If he made it to the freeway, it could add potential contact with the state's highway patrol. The only law he likely *wouldn't* see would be the Texas Rangers—and he had one of them riding in his shotgun seat.

With half a block to spare, he chose the right-hand turn. Given the hour, Bolan knew downtown would have more traffic on the streets, people returning home from restaurants, concerts and theaters, whatever. More police patrols, for sure, keeping an eye on high-rent stores and offices. If he could lead the hunters south, then west toward the San Antonio River, the street map he'd memorized during his flight told Bolan he would find dead ground, where they could stop and settle it.

The hunters hadn't lost Bolan when he had turned onto South Bowie, but they hadn't started shooting, either. That was good news, and he wasted no time trying to interpret it.

"Who's likely to be tracking you?" he asked his passenger.

She answered with a question of her own. "What were you told about this deal?"

"The basics. Ridgway and the NTR."

"Okay. It could be either one of them, assuming there's a difference. Lamar won't soil his hands, but he could give the order. Might demand a video, for his enjoyment over cocktails later."

"Not police," Bolan confirmed.

"No lights or sirens," she replied. "No way."

That made it easier. At the beginning of his one-man war against the Mafia, Bolan had drawn a line he would never cross. When dealing with police at any level, in any given situation, he would not use deadly force. Whether they qualified as heroes or were nothing more than thugs in uniform, he treated law enforcement officers as soldiers on the same side. Bolan would not spill their blood, even in self-defense.

He'd sent a few to prison, sure, but that was something else entirely.

Mercenary killers, on the other hand, were fair game whenever and wherever they crossed paths with the Executioner.

South Bowie reached East Commerce Street, and Bolan took a right there, racing west to catch South Alamo. The chase car hung in there, trying to ride his bumper, but the lighter RAV4 kept a few car lengths between them, weaving just enough to cut the hunters off from passing by on either side, where they could get a clean shot at the smaller SUV.

Not yet.

The farther they could go without a shot fired or a squad car joining in the chase, the better Bolan liked it. They would have their showdown soon enough, in true Wild West tradition, more or less.

South Alamo took Bolan and Granger on a long southwestern swing through tree-lined residential areas, rolling inexorably toward the river and a strip of warehouses that served its traffic. There were few pedestrians around as they passed by darkened homes, some with the flicker of a television screen behind drawn curtains, others with their occupants asleep before another workday in the city. Maybe roaring engines caused a ripple in their dreams, but Bolan was satisfied to spare them from a running firefight.

"Gaining," Granger cautioned. Nothing that his rearview hadn't shown him.

"Just a little longer," he replied.

"Why aren't they shooting?"

"Maybe someone wants to have a word with you."

"That's not going to happen."

Not if I can help it, Bolan thought, and squeezed a bit more speed from the Toyota's growling engine.

He could see a bridge across the river coming up, a strip mall to his left once they'd crossed it and a factory of some kind to his right, with giant stacks and at least a dozen semi-trailers lined up outside, waiting for loads. A triple set of railroad tracks ran through the plant and disappeared beneath an elevated walkway. A sign atop the tallest portion of the factory read Pioneer. Another, set above the three tall stacks, read White Wings.

Bolan didn't have a clue what was produced there, and he didn't care. The place was obviously closed, no cars in the employees' parking lot. Tapping the RAV4's brake pedal, he swung in off the street and rolled across the lot, which was lit by bright halogen lights.

"HE'S STOPPING HERE? What the hell's he thinkin'?" Jesse Folsom asked.

"How the hell should I know?" Bryar Haskin snapped. "Let's take 'em while we can."

"Some kinda trick," suggested Jackson.

"Doesn't matter." Haskin jacked a round into his shotgun's chamber. "Now he's off the road, we got 'im."

"Light 'em up!" said Jimmy Don Bodine.

"Hold off on that," Haskin commanded. "Don't forget Kent wants 'em both alive, if possible."

"If possible." The echo came from Jackson. "Leaves a lotta wiggle room."

"You screw this up," said Haskin, "you'll be wigglin' when he hooks your nuts up to that hand-crank generator with some alligator clips."

Jackson had no response to that, and it was just as well. Folsom, at the Yukon's wheel, swung in behind the black Toyota, chasing it across the mostly empty parking lot, back toward a row of semitrailers lined up closer to the factory. Haskin had no idea why their intended prey would trap himself that way, instead of staying on South Alamo, maybe trying to lose them on the Pan Am Expressway farther west, but he didn't plan to look a gift horse in the mouth.

"C'mon!" he barked at Folsom. "Catch 'em, damn it!"

"Workin' on it," Jesse answered back, accelerating with a squeal of tires on asphalt.

Haskin had no clue who was driving the Toyota, but it stood to reason that the lady Ranger would be armed. A pistol only, since he'd seen her walking empty-handed at the Alamo, unlikely that she'd have some kind of tiny submachine gun underneath her leather jacket. Could be damn near anything inside the fleeing SUV, though, so they'd have to hit it hard and fast, before the stranger at the wheel could start unloading on them.

"Hey! You're losin' it," warned Haskin, as the RAV4 swerved around behind semis, ducking out of sight.

"No place for 'em to go back there," Folsom assured him. "Ain't no exit from the lot on that side."

"You'd better hope not. If they get away—"

"You worry too much," Folsom answered, almost sneering.

Haskin fought an urge to punch him, the worst thing Haskin could do when they were doing close to sixty miles per hour. If Folsom crashed the Yukon, it would be Haskin's ass when Kent heard how their targets had wriggled through the net.

Haskin had expected the Toyota's driver to swing back around, upon discovering that he couldn't escape the parking lot, but there was no sign of the RAV4 yet. It was a big lot, sure, but not *that* big. You couldn't lose an SUV, unless—

"Hold up!" he ordered.

Folsom shot a sidelong glance his way.

"They're layin' for us!" Haskin blurted, but his driver didn't get the message. They kept rolling, passed the nearest semi-trailer, turning left to follow the Toyota. Haskin didn't see the other car at first, imagined that its wheelman must have found an exit from the big lot after all or maybe plowed straight through the shrubbery that lined it on the west. He was about to say so, when a sudden blaze of high beams blinded him. He raised one hand to shield his eyes.

"Goddamn it!"

The words were barely out before a bullet drilled through their windshield, clipped the rearview mirror from its post and dropped it into Haskin's lap. Folsom was cursing like a sailor with his pants on fire, spinning the Yukon's wheel, as more slugs hit the SUV, pounding its body like the sharp blows of a sledgehammer.

BOLAN HAD RACED around the line of semitrailers, running almost to its end before he whipped the RAV4 through a rocking bootlegger's turn. It wasn't too hard, once taught the trick, using the hand brake and accelerator in collaboration, power steering helping out. With an SUV there was a risk of tipping over, but he had kept them upright—though not without eliciting a little gasp from Adlene Granger.

"Out!" he snapped, when they were barely settled, reaching toward the backseat for his hidden Colt AR-15. She bailed from the passenger's side. He had already doused the domes, but a pool of light still glowed beneath the dashboard with the SUV's doors open. Not enough to matter for his purposes, as Bolan crouched behind his open driver's door and Granger found her cover in between two massive semis.

Any second now…

The chase car roared into view right on schedule, head-lights lancing toward the parked RAV4. They had to see it, but the black car sitting there, stopped dead and going nowhere, would confuse them long enough for Bolan to begin the fight on his own terms. A slim advantage, when he guessed they were outnumbered two to one, at least, but he would take what he could get.

Which, at the moment, was a blast of high beams for the chase car's driver, followed by a clean shot through its tinted windshield. Bolan didn't count on hitting anyone with that first round, but it did have the desired effect, forcing the larger SUV to swerve away from him, tires screeching on the asphalt as its wheelman panicked.

Bolan tracked the Yukon with his rifle sights, squeezed off another round that sent its left-front tire into a wallowing rumble, the rim biting blacktop. That didn't help the driver with control, but he still managed not to flip it, trying to put space between himself and Bolan as he rolled off toward the tall white stacks on the far side of the parking lot.

Looking for cover, Bolan realized, and he was determined not to let them reach it. Breaking from his own partial con-cealment, after switching off the Toyota's headlights, Bolan sprinted in pursuit of the Yukon. He was the hunter now, whether the Yukon's occupants knew it or not. The game had turned around on them, but there was no change in the stakes.

Still life or death.

Before his targets reached the three silo stacks, Bolan stopped short, lined up his shot and punched a double-tap through the retreating 4x4's rear window. Glass imploded, and he thought he heard a man cry out; whether in pain or mere surprise, he couldn't say. Then the SUV changed course again, now rolling toward a fence and wall of shrubbery that screened the parking lot's west end.

Better.

Over there, the only cover waiting for them was the vehicle they had arrived in. They could try to scale the fence and run away, but that would place them with their backs toward Bolan, no hands free for fighting while they made the climb. He could shoot sitting ducks all night, though Bolan hoped to wrap this up without much wasted time.

And if he had a chance to quiz one of his enemies, so much the better.

The Yukon rolled on toward the fence, then veered off to the right. That placed the driver's side away from Bolan, and he saw the doors fly open, dome lights glaring briefly until they were shut once more. It looked like four men piling out, none seemingly impaired, going to ground behind the full-size SUV.

Now *Bolan* was in the open and in danger as they started firing—one from each end of the Yukon, one underneath it and one blasting directly through the SUV, its back windows both rolled down.

Not good.

His opposition had two shotguns and two rifles, both feeding the standard 5.56 mm NATO ammunition by their sound. One hit from any of those guns could be enough to finish him. Whether they scored with buckshot or one of the NATO tumblers traveling at 3,100 feet per second, either would create catastrophic damage upon impact with flesh and bone.

He hit the deck and rolled, scrabbling away to his left, toward the last semitrailer in line. It stood some fifty yards from the Yukon, easy pickings with his AR-15, but Bolan still had two problems.

He needed a line on his targets, of course.

And he had to reach cover alive.

"Get out! Out! Out!" Bryar Haskin shouted, shoving Folsom when the driver moved too slowly to suit him.

"Jesus, man! I'm go—" Folsom's words were cut off as he spilled from the Yukon, Haskin crowding out behind him on the driver's side, the steering wheel bruising his ribs. He nearly stepped on Jesse as he fell.

Cursing a blue streak, Folsom kicked back at him, almost brought him down, and in the process accidentally saved Haskin's life.

The impact made Haskin stumble and drop to one knee just as a bullet smashed the Yukon's right-front window, passing within an inch of Haskin's head. He could have sworn he felt it graze his hair before it whispered off into the darkness. Another bullet hit the open driver's door a heartbeat later, spraying Haskin's face and neck with jagged bits of steel and plastic.

"Agh!"

He slammed the door behind him, cutting off the Yukon's dome lights, staying low in case the rifleman kept shooting through the SUV.

"Shoot back!" he ordered. "What in hell'd we bring these guns for, anyway?"

It took another second, but his boys got in the spirit of the thing, returning fire. Haskin angled his Ithaca across the Yukon's hood and fired a blast toward the parking lot, seeing a figure drop and roll out there but having no idea if he'd been hit. Doubtful, in the confusion, with his own guys firing wild and ducking back before a lucky shot could pick them off.

Speaking of which, Haskin felt too exposed aiming across the Yukon's nose, so he went prone and aimed his twelve-gauge underneath the SUV. Not hiding, get that straight; being crafty, with a bid to cut their adversary's legs from under him, leaving him helpless on the blacktop. Might have worked, too, but it seemed as if the guy was gone now. Likely over by the nearest of the semitrailers, lining up another shot.

And what about the lady Ranger? Where was she?

Haskin had little time to think about it, as his first guess was confirmed. A muzzle-flash winked at him from the darkened space between two trailers, fifty yards or so away, and Haskin heard slugs punching through the Yukon's right-front fender, hammering the engine.

Shit!

Damned inconvenient for them if they had to leave their

ride behind, although its registration wouldn't lead investigators anywhere. That was the beauty of a holding company, something Haskin had heard about but never really understood until it was explained to him in simple terms, of late—a paper trail that led the cops in circles without yielding any information that could hang him or his friends if anything went wrong.

Like now.

As for escaping, they could always take the other guy's Toyota once they'd finished with him. And the Ranger. Couldn't forget her, since she'd started this whole fouled-up business in the first place. Kent still wanted her alive, but Haskin wasn't sure he could deliver on that order, given how things stood right now.

How long before the shooting brought a prowl car, followed by a SWAT team? He wasn't sure, but every passing minute made their prospects worse. He tried to picture Kent's reaction if they all wound up in jail but didn't like where that was going, so he pushed the image out of mind.

More bullets slapped at the Yukon. "We gotta flush that bastard out of there," Haskin told his men.

"Go for it," Jackson answered, making no attempt to move.

"You scared of goin' out there?" Haskin challenged him.

"Damn right!"

"Well guess what?" Haskin snarled, jabbing his shotgun's muzzle into Jackson's ribs. "You're goin' anyhow."

"Son of a bitch!"

"Move it!"

Still cursing, Jackson waddled toward the Yukon's tailgate, braced himself and charged into the open, firing as he ran. And covered all of ten feet, maybe less, before a bullet brought him down.

And that left three.

BOLAN HAD DROPPED the runner with a head shot, easy, and his friends were clearly having second thoughts about an all-out rush to finish it. He glanced back toward the RAV4, saw no sign of Granger and hoped she'd keep it that way while he finished up the skirmish. Bolan's chance of capturing a shooter for interrogation seemed less likely now, but any hope remaining would require the gunmen to be driven out from under cover, where he'd have an opportunity to pick and choose.

How best to do it?

While they popped off wasted rounds—some scoring hits on semis, others squandered on thin air—he sighted on the SUV's fuel tank. The Yukon carried twenty-six gallons of gasoline when it was filled to the brim, but Bolan didn't need a full tank for his purposes. Three rounds fired through the right-rear quarter panel were enough to set it dribbling, a small lake forming underneath the vehicle.

Now all he needed was a spark.

The cornered gunmen didn't seem to see where he was going with it, firing back at Bolan for the sake of making noise, the nearest of their shots missing him by two feet or more. Meanwhile he concentrated on the Yukon's right-rear wheel. He flattened its tire with one shot, then directed three more at the rim, trying to strike a spark.

He was rewarded by a puff of flame, the gas fumes catching, then the spilled gas on the blacktop came alight and sent its head back to the leaking fuel tank. Bolan waited for combustion, heard one of his hidden enemies growl out a warning to the others, but it came too late. The gas tank blew, lifting the Yukon's rear end on a bright cushion of fire, some six to eight feet off the ground.

That sent them running. One man, in flames, broke out to his left with staggered steps, wailing, then dropped to hands and knees, trying to roll the fire out as it bit into his flesh. His two companions ran the other way, toward the silo stacks, firing in Bolan's general direction as they fled.

A pistol cracked from somewhere to his right, distracting Bolan for a split second before he made it out as a .45. Granger was pitching in to help, her second shot dropping the forward runner in a boneless sprawl. His sidekick skidded to a halt, couldn't decide which way to turn his automatic rifle, so he swept the parking lot at large with crackling fire, hoping to score a lucky hit. He drew more fire from Granger, off the mark this time, and ran toward the stacks again.

They'd lose him there, and Bolan couldn't have that, even if he gave up the chance for an interrogation. Lining up his shot, be put a round between the shooter's shoulder blades, the impact lifting Bolan's target and propelling him some six or seven feet, shoes churning empty air. He landed facedown on the asphalt, rifle skittering away from lifeless fingers, and lay still.

All done…except that one of them was still alive and whimpering.

Bolan crossed to stand by the shooter who had been on fire a moment earlier. Reached down to pluck a pistol from the burned man's belt and to toss it out of reach, into the shadows. Crouching down beside him, breathing through his mouth to minimize the stench of roasted flesh, Bolan asked, "Who sent you after us?"

"You…get…nothin'…from…me."

"A name, that's all," Bolan replied. "You don't owe them a thing."

"What the hell…do you…know?" Wheezing smoke came from the man's mouth and nose.

"I'm guessing Crockett," Bolan said.

"Screw…you."

"Or maybe Ridgway?"

One eye widened slightly, or the other might have narrowed. With the scorching on the shooter's face, Bolan couldn't be sure. A wink? He doubted it. More likely pain, sending a tremor through seared flesh.

"So, nothing?"

"Uh…uh."

"Okay then."

He rose, backed off a pace and plugged a mercy round into the shooter's blackened forehead.

"Jesus God!"

And turned to find the Ranger watching him, a grim expression on her face.

"We're done here," Bolan told her. "Time to go."

4

"You blew that guy away like it was nothing," Adlene Granger said.

"You saw him," Bolan answered. "He was suffering."

"So that was mercy?"

"Partly."

"What does that mean?"

"You'll agree we couldn't help him, right? And who knows when the first responders might arrive."

"We could have called it in anonymously."

"Then what? If they saved him, what comes next? You want him talking to police, or to whoever sent him and his buddies after you?"

"How do I know that they weren't after you?" she challenged.

Bolan ticked the points off on his fingers. "First, nobody knows me here. Second, there's no way they could know who was specifically coming to meet with you. Third, the Yukon had a set of Texas plates and wasn't rented. Fourth—"

"All right, I get it."

They were rolling north on Dwyer Avenue, circling back toward Alamo Plaza and Granger's car, left in the parking lot when they had ducked the shooters there. Taking their time, they might have been returning from a late date, taking in a movie.

Or a massacre.

"Okay, so someone set me up." Her voice was grim.

"Not necessarily," Bolan replied.

"How's that?"

"Did you tell anyone about our meeting?"

"Absolutely not."

"Then no one could have leaked it. They've been trailing you. You missed it. These things happen."

"Trailing me. Damn it!"

"They obviously knew your brother. Maybe they had time to check his cell phone after he was—"

"Killed. Go on."

"But even if they didn't, you're a logical connection. Sister, law enforcement, who else would he talk to?"

"No one."

"What's your next move?" Bolan asked her.

"Try to stay alive, I guess. How's that?"

"When are you back on duty?"

"After Jerod's funeral. I'm on bereavement leave."

"About the funeral…"

"Oh, God. Don't tell me."

"It's the first place that they'd look for you, after your home."

"God *damn* it! So, I can't go home and can't bury my brother? That's just frickin' great!"

"You can report what's happened. See about protective custody."

"For life? Get serious. You're only here because I couldn't trust the locals or my own department."

"What, then?" Bolan asked.

"Looks like I'll be a fugitive."

"I hate to mention this," said Bolan, "but you dropped one of those guys back there."

"He was escaping. Sue me."

"I was thinking of ballistics."

Granger thought about that for a moment, then replied, "No problem. Texas doesn't have a database of cartridges or slugs from law enforcement weapons. Maryland tried that, a few years back, and ditched it. Said the deal was too expensive and had never solved a crime."

"So, what's your next move?"

After more thought, then she said, "How 'bout I stick with you?"

Now it was Bolan's turn to think. He hadn't come to Texas looking for a sidekick, only information that would clarify the situation and, if need be, point him toward potential targets. Granted, local expertise might come in handy, but he didn't want to take responsibility for Adlene Granger's safety.

Or was it too late to make that call?

"You've seen the way I work," he said. "It just gets worse from here."

"You're not a normal Fed, I take it," almost smiling as she spoke.

"Not even close."

"Some kind of spook then."

"More or less."

"I shouldn't push it, right?"

"Good call."

"You're not collecting evidence to build a case."

"Correct."

"A little Texas frontier justice, maybe?"

Bolan let that pass. They were a mile out from the Alamo.

"Look," she continued. "All I'm saying is, I know what fighting's all about. Tonight wasn't first blood for me."

"I've seen your file," Bolan informed her.

"Oh? Well then." A brief hesitation followed. "So I *have* a file? In Washington, I mean?"

"Who doesn't?"

"Right. We're good to go then?"

"Sergeant Granger—"

"Adlene," she corrected him. "First date and we're already shooting people. May as well be on a first-name basis."

Bolan had to smile at that. "Adlene, I normally don't work with partners."

"You're a loner, eh? Afraid I'll slow you down and get all dewy-eyed? I thought you'd seen my file."

"I have."

"Then you know that I spent two years in the sand. It wasn't a vacation, and I'm not a clinging vine."

"If anything goes wrong—"

"I'm on my own. Got it."

Another beat passed, before he said, "You have some information for me?"

"Sketchy. Jerod didn't want to tell me too much on the phone. I got a name and an affiliation, but it just might get us started."

"What's the name?"

"Craig Walraven. I'd never heard of him before. Have you?"

"First time for me, as well."

"He works for Lone Star, meaning Ridgway, but his last gig was a mouthful. Something with the National Nuclear Security Administration's Office of Fissile Material Disposition."

And there it was. The linkup to a possible catastrophe.

Tom Green County, Texas

IN KENT LUTTRELL'S OPINION, the only thing worse than receiving bad news was passing it on to his boss. It was a part of life sometimes, but he had learned from grim experience that Waylon Crockett liked his news served sunny-side up, not scrambled and burnt to a crisp. He especially wouldn't like hearing that plans to secure the great coup of a lifetime had failed like a cheap retread tire on a hot desert highway.

He wouldn't be happy at all.

The call from San Antonio had come in moments earlier, one of Luttrell's men phoning to alert him that the pickup had unraveled. Gone to hell would be more like it, since the two marks had not simply slipped away from Bryar Haskin's team. The Ranger and her pal, whoever he might be, had slaughtered four good men—well, not *that* good, apparently—and left them for the cops to find. Now he would have to sweat it out, waiting to see if any of them could be traced back to the New Texas Republic.

He assumed the FBI and ATF had lists of the Republic's members. Those who occupied the compound; staffers at the tiny storefront offices in Dallas, Houston and El Paso; likely anyone who'd shown up at a public rally since the movement started. That was standard for the thought police: collecting names, addresses, phone numbers, affiliations.

If they weren't eavesdropping on the NTR's phone lines, Kent would have been amazed. Prepaid cell phones helped a little, and he had a scrambler on the compound's landline, but when cameras on satellites could read your lips from outer space, was anything or anyone truly secure?

Fat chance.

Quit stalling. Breaking bad news to the boss was like yanking a Band-Aid off a hairy arm. The more slowly done, the worse it stung.

Luttrell left his small bungalow and walked across the compound to a larger one, Crockett's combination living quarters and command post. Kent knocked once and waited in the moonlight until Crockett made his slow way to the door. It opened, and he saw that Crockett had a pistol in his hand, prepared for trouble even here and now.

"They called?"

Luttrell nodded. "It isn't good."

"Awright. Get in here." He sounded weary. When the door had closed behind him, Crockett ordered, "Tell me."

For a second Luttrell thought about that old expression: *Shoot the messenger.* He shrugged it off and said, "Something went wrong. I don't have any details yet, except the team went down."

Crockett blinked once. "All four of 'em?"

"All four."

"What about the pigeons?"

"Flew the coop. They're in the wind."

"No way to track them?"

"I've got people sitting on her house and on the mortuary where they took her brother. We'll hear something if she calls headquarters. Otherwise…"

"We're screwed."

"We'll have to wait and see."

"While she's out there running her mouth."

"It doesn't feel that way to me," Luttrell replied. "We know she hasn't tipped the DPS."

Meaning the Texas Department of Public Safety, an umbrella unit based in Austin, covering the Texas Rangers and the Texas Highway Patrol, the state's Criminal Investigations Division, plus its Intelligence and Counterterrorism Division. They had that side covered and would know if something broke.

"And what about the Feds?" asked Crockett.

"I can't swear she hasn't called them, but the deal tonight wasn't their style. They wouldn't dust Haskin and his boys then run away. We'd see them on the tube, hyping their victory. They'd be out at the gate with warrants."

Nodding, Crockett said, "Okay then. Who?"

"You'll know as soon as I do," said Luttrell.

"You'd better make it quick. I gotta go wake up The Man."

Dallas, Texas

HALF PAST 2:00 A.M. and Simon Coetzee had been asleep just long enough to slide into a dream of hunting humans. His beloved South African homeland may have turned into a cesspool, but at night, in dreams, Coetzee did his part to cleanse it.

This morning, he was just about to squeeze the trigger on his .460 Weatherby Magnum rifle when the shrilling telephone beside his bed jarred Coetzee out of Africa and back to Texas in a bitter rush of disappointment.

"Yes?"

"It's me," the caller said, expecting him to recognize the voice.

Which, of course, Coetzee did. "You know what time it is?"

"Late. Early. I don't know. We got a problem."

"Scramble this," said Coetzee, stretching out an arm to press a button at the base of his bedside phone. A red light glowed in response.

"Okay, ready," Waylon Crockett told him from the other end.

"All right. What is it?"

"I toldja 'bout that Ranger and her brother. Granger?"

"Yes. You were supposed to handle her." Coetzee, after all, had taken care of Jerod Granger. Such a relatively simple thing.

"Um, well…somethin' went wrong," said Crockett.

"Oh?"

"She met this other guy…and, um…my boys moved in on 'em…but, um…well, shit. My guys are dead."

"How many?"

"Four."

Coetzee inhaled, held it, willing his anger to subside. Eyes closed, in darkness, he waited for the throbbing in his temples to recede.

"You there?" asked Crockett.

"Where else would I be?"

"Dunno. I thought—"

"You're telling me this woman and a man you've never seen before took out four of your men."

"Tha's right."

"And I assume that the police are now involved?"

"Um, yeah."

"Can these four be identified?"

"They wouldn't have I.D. on 'em," said Crockett. "We got rid of all that when we came out as a sovereign nation under God. No driver's licenses or social insecurity, nothin' like that."

"Plastic?"

"Say what?"

"Would they have credit cards? For petrol or whatever?"

"Petrol?"

"Gasoline."

"Nope. We're completely off the grid. All cash and carry."

Thank heavens for small favors. "That leaves fingerprints," said Coetzee.

"Um…well…a couple of 'em mighta been inside a time or two."

"Meaning in prison."

"Or a county lockup. Somethin'."

"So their prints are in the system then."

"I reckon so."

"And can be traced to you."

"Well now, our membership is confidential."

"In this day and age?" Coetzee smiled bitterly in the darkness. "Feel free to deceive yourself if it amuses you but *never* lie to me."

"I guess the Feds might recognize 'em."

"And when they come knocking, you can easily explain that these four brainless yokels *were* your members on a previous occasion, but you sacked them for erratic and irrational behavior. You have no idea what they've been up to since you parted company. Of course you'd love to help with the investigation, but you have no useful information."

"That might work."

"Can you remember all of that?"

"I ain't an idjit," Crockett bristled.

"I keep waiting for some evidence of that," Coetzee replied.

"Hey, now—"

"You realize I'll have to pass this news upstairs."

"Uh-huh."

"It won't be well received."

"I'll make it right. You tell him not to worry. We're already lookin' for the two of 'em."

"See that you get it right this time," said Coetzee, then he cut the link.

Preston Hollow, Dallas

LAMAR RIDGWAY WAS not awakened by a telephone. He left that inconvenience to his butler, who had served him for the better part of thirty years without complaint. In short, he knew his place. The gentle tap on Ridgway's bedroom door was followed by the butler's deep voice, softly calling out his name.

"What is it, Fabius?"

"You've got a phone call, sir."

Sweet Jesus! "Awright, bring it in."

The butler entered, strode with purpose toward the king-size bed, and passed the cordless phone to Ridgway from a white-gloved hand. "I'll just be right outside, sir."

"Hmm." Ridgway sat waiting for the bedroom door to close, before he raised the phone and said, "Better be good."

"It's not, sir." Simon Coetzee, Ridgway's master of security for Lone Star Petroleum and Aerospace Technology.

"Awright then. Don't keep me hangin'."

Coetzee didn't ask if they were scrambled. He'd installed Ridgway's elaborate home security system, knew it inside out.

"It's Crockett," he began. "This business with the Texas Ranger and her brother."

"Christ, is that still draggin' on?"

"They planned to finish it this evening, sir. Unfortunately—"

"They screwed up?"

"Four dead, all Crockett's men. The woman and her contact still remain at large."

"This contact…"

"Male, identity unknown. We'll check flights into San Antonio, of course, sir."

"But you likely won't get squat. On top of which, he coulda drove in, even rode in on a goddamn bus."

"Yes, sir."

"We're close, Simon. You *know* how friggin' close we are."

"I do, sir."

"I don't want anybody pissin' on my dream."

"They won't, sir."

"Seems to me they're pretty goddamn close to doin' it right now."

"I won't allow that, sir."

"See that you don't."

"No, sir."

"You're like a son to me," said Ridgway. "Like the son I never had."

A heartbeat's silence came on the other end. "Thank you, sir," Coetzee said.

"And a father dreads the day when he has to bury his child."

Ridgway ended the call. Let Coetzee chew on that a while. Lamar called out toward the bedroom door, "I'm done! Come get the goddamn phone!"

Fabius entered, took the instrument, and wished Ridgway a restful night.

"Too late for that," the oil man grumbled, as he burrowed back into his sheets and drew the quilted comforter up to his double chin.

Small minds had hampered Ridgway all his life, trying to hold him back. In school before he'd left the seventh grade, small-minded teachers had tried to pigeonhole him, telling him that he would never amount to a fart in a cyclone.

His parents and their parson had tried to sell him the same message, binding him to a hardscrabble farm and a church built on strict "thou shalt nots." Ridgway had kicked over the traces, gone out on his own and proved them wrong. In spades.

Once he was rich as Croesus—no, scratch that; *richer* than Croesus or the Lord Himself—small minds kept after him in other ways. They told him that he should concentrate on oil and gas, stick with the things he knew, where he had proven his ability. Don't branch out into other fields and least of all space exploration. What did any Texas oil man with a sixth-grade education know about the friggin' moon and stars beyond it?

Next to nothing, granted. But he had money to burn, enough to buy the brains that *did* know all about the universe and rockets, astrophysics, interplanetary travel—name your poison. And he knew some other things, as well.

Ridgway knew that his country had been losing ground for decades—hell, for generations. Ever since the last world war, when Roosevelt and Truman let Joe Stalin gobble up half of the world without a fight. The great U.S. of A. had been declining ever since, with racial integration and affirmative action, gay rights and abortion, losing wars all over Asia and the Middle East.

He'd done his best to save America, bankrolling groups that stood against the long slide into socialism's Sodom and Gomorrah, but he'd finally admitted to himself that they were beaten. His United States, the one he loved, was circling the drain.

And it was time to start from scratch.

He'd be goddamned if some inept redneck would spoil it now.

You want a job done right, a small voice in his head reminded him, *do it yourself.*

San Antonio

CONGRESS HAD CREATED the National Nuclear Security Administration in 2000, following the scandal that had enveloped Dr. Wen Ho Lee and the Los Alamos National Laboratory. Lee had been accused of passing secrets about America's nuclear arsenal to the People's Republic of China, pleading guilty on one of fifty-nine charges, then turned around and won a $1.6 million defamation judgment from the Feds and various media networks. The trial judge later apologized to Dr. Lee and blasted the justice department for suppressing and mishandling evidence.

In spite of that confusing episode—or possibly because of it—the NNSA was created within the U.S. Department of Energy, with the goal of both reducing the threat caused by nuclear weapons worldwide, and of supporting America's endeavors in developing and managing safe, effective nuclear technology.

Simple.

The NNSA's Office of Fissile Material Disposition was responsible for disposing of excess plutonium and highly enriched uranium. Both materials, commonly used in weapons of mass destruction, were collected by the OFMD and converted for peaceful use as commercial nuclear reactor fuel. In November 2007, collection of fissile material was expanded from America to include surplus plutonium from Russia.

And now, it seemed, the OFMD might have sprung a leak.

"This Walraven," said Bolan. "What's his job at Lone Star?"

"Jerod didn't have a chance to tell me," Adlene Granger answered. "When I did a Google search, I found out that he has a Ph.D. from MIT in nuclear physics. He's published papers, but I couldn't understand the titles, let alone the gist of them."

"Smart money says he works for Lone Star's aerospace division," Bolan said.

"He'd fit right in," Granger replied. "They hired a slew of NASA people when the agency was laying off their rocket scientists. A guy named George Roth runs the show. They claim to have a shuttle up and running, ready for commercial flights within a year or so."

"Did your brother say that Ridgway *has* fissile material, or that he's trying to acquire it?" Bolan asked.

"We never got that far. He was supposed to have some files, but they were gone when the police found him in Lubbock."

"And he worked for Lone Star?"

"Right. In their accounting department."

"Where he could have stumbled onto something classified, while he was balancing the books."

"Makes sense to me," Granger agreed.

They were rolling east on Houston Street, two blocks from Alamo Plaza. Bolan had been watching for patrol cars, marked or otherwise. Driving a circuit of the plaza, he saw nothing to suggest police had staked it out. Nor, it appeared, had any reinforcements turned out for the team that they'd eliminated, to watch Granger's Dodge Avenger.

He pulled into the parking lot and stopped beside the Dodge. Granger already had her keys in one hand, pistol in the other.

"This is it," he told her. "Time to choose whether you're in or out."

"They killed my brother," she replied.

Bolan cut to the chase. "You want to join him?"

"What?"

"You need to understand that there's a chance you might not walk away from this. And if you do, the Rangers may not want you back."

"I'll take my chances."

"Then we need to get you organized. First thing, you can't go home."

"I get that."

"You may need a change of clothes, gas up your ride, whatever."

"So I'll shop."

"No credit cards. No bank withdrawals."

"Damn it!"

"Here." He took a wad of greenbacks from his pocket, handing it to Granger.

"What's this?"

"Just a little contribution from the war chest."

"I don't need a sugar daddy."

"And I'm not applying for the job," he said. "The money's dirty, but it spends the same."

"So you're a robber, too?"

"Let's say I got it from a cartel boss who didn't need it anymore."

"You always play for keeps?"

"Is there another way?"

"Okay. What's next?"

"We pay a call on Mr. Walraven."

5

Craig Walraven always woke at dawn. No matter where he was, what he was doing or how late he'd worked the night before, he could not sleep past sunrise. It was a quirk he'd never really understood but had learned to live with, since he had no other choice. Get up and get a jump on any competition, any trouble that the new day held in store.

This morning, as his habit was, he listened to the news on the radio while showering. He favored station KRLD out of Dallas, right next door to Arlington, because it was an all-news station, the equivalent of CNN without the talking heads and the annoying, often misspelled headlines crawling endlessly across the bottom of the television screen. He turned up the volume to make it audible over the drumming of his shower, and because he had no neighbors to complain.

The good life. Finally.

Walraven would not have said that his years of mostly desk-bound labor with the National Nuclear Security Administration's Office of Fissile Material Disposition had been wasted. If not for that phase of his life, he would not have transcended the workaday drudgery that held so many others of his age and educational background in thrall. He might have been stuck in some university laboratory, working on some project that would ultimately make the institution richer and more famous, while he toiled in anonymity for the academic equivalent of minimum wage.

Instead, he'd seen an opportunity—or rather had one set before him on a silver platter—and he'd grabbed it. He was wealthy now, beyond his former wildest dreams; although, of course, such things were always relative. He'd never be a billionaire, like some folks he could name offhand. But at the not-so-tender age of forty-three, he had three-quarters of a million dollars in an offshore bank account, and more was rolling in each month.

On top of which, he had a chance to change the world.

It was a good life, certainly. But how long would it last?

Later, after The Change, would he be as valued as he was today? Or would he suddenly become disposable? Walraven had accepted certain promises on faith but knew full well that ultrawealthy people often changed their minds and changed directions without thinking of the consequences for the little people crushed beneath their feet. Therefore, he had prepared an exit strategy, had nearly all the pieces set in place, ready for use in an emergency, should one arise.

The main part of his work, he understood, was quickly coming to an end. In fact, his underlings and the technicians he had trained could likely get along without him now. If promises were broken, all he needed was a moment's warning. He had already accumulated passports, credit cards and other documents in two new names, and last month had secured a rental property outside of Auckland, on New Zealand's North Island.

Whatever happened once he left, Walraven thought that half a world away from Texas should be far enough to keep him safe.

KRLD was a CBS affiliate. As Walraven turned off the shower, news anchor Mike Rogers was giving details of a shooting in San Antonio. It sounded like a bloody business—four men dead, all armed with heavy weapons—but it wasn't anything unusual for Texas. For all of the governor's tough talk on law and order, the pride he took in executing prison inmates, Texas had still logged over one hundred thousand violent crimes a year, including murders, rapes, aggravated assaults and armed robberies.

Walraven toweled himself dry, standing under the bathroom's heat lamp, warm tiles beneath his feet. In his bedroom, Walraven had laid out his clothes for the day: a Ralph Lauren broadcloth sport shirt, Brooks Brothers slacks and Florsheim penny loafers. No tie today, since he'd be spending most of his time inside a radiation suit, and comfort mattered.

When he'd finished dressing, Walraven began to prepare a leisurely breakfast. Another benefit of rising with the dawn was that he rarely had to rush in the morning. No crude meals prepared in haste and bolted down to fuel a storm of indigestion. He was not exactly a gourmet but had the skill to please himself—and the occasional young woman who might join him for a little taste of heaven.

He was warming up a skillet when the doorbell rang. Frowning, Walraven turned off the stove and made his way to the front door. He blinked in surprise as he peered through the peephole, recognizing a familiar face.

The frown was still in place as he opened the door and said, "I didn't hear your car."

BOLAN'S HIGHWAY MAP told him that Arlington lay 231 miles north of San Antonio, as the turkey buzzard flies. He rolled north on Interstate 35, quickly discovering why the segment of it between San Antonio and Austin is considered to be among the most congested stretches of highway in the American interstate system.

One of the country's major NAFTA corridors, it hums with big rigs day and night, bearing all manner of cargo to and from Mexico. In Austin proper, where it's known as the Interregional Highway, I-35 narrows from eight lanes to four, slowing the pace of heavy traffic that much more.

The long drive gave Bolan time to think, while Adlene Granger alternately dozed in the passenger's seat or watched the flatland of Texas slide past her window. Daylight overtook them as they entered Waco, scene of the 1993 Branch Davidian siege and a continuing source of criticism for the Feds.

Bolan remembered it, of course—who could forget the images of conflagration running live on television, then repeated endlessly?—and he supposed there had been fault enough to go around on both sides. An apocalyptic cult, members armed to the teeth and prepared to die for their charismatic leader, squaring off against authority composed in equal parts of arrogance and righteous indignation. It had fired a generation of rebellion, plots and insurrection, private armies on the march.

And it obviously wasn't over yet.

Once they had passed Fort Worth Spinks Airport, Bolan left the interstate and pulled onto a rural highway known as Farm-to-Market 1187, winding his way toward Craig Walraven's home near the Tierra Verde Golf Club.

Living in the rural lap of luxury.

As he was turning off the interstate and heading eastward, Granger broke the silence. "So, our theory is that Walraven's been cooking up a nuke for Ridgway?"

"Not impossible," Bolan replied. "We know fissile material's been disappearing since the fifties. Some out of labs, but most goes missing in transit. I read that something like three tons of weapons-grade uranium and plutonium sold to foreign allies over the years—mostly for use as fuel in reactors—has yet to be accounted for. You only need thirty-five *pounds* of uranium-235 to build a nuclear bomb, nine pounds of plutonium."

"So there's enough floating around out there, somewhere, to make…what? Almost two hundred uranium bombs?"

"At least," Bolan replied. "Closer to seven hundred if it was all plutonium."

"That's pretty freakin' grim."

"The good news is, nobody's detonated one so far," he said. No point in telling her how close a few had come.

Walraven's place was near the intersection of Mansfield Highway and Gertie Barrett Road, a rambling ranch-style home set on four acres of land. There was a sleek gray BMW 5 Series Gran Turismo in the driveway, but no sign of lookouts on the property. Bolan parked behind the import, pocketed the RAV4's key and stepped out of the SUV into bright Texas sunshine.

"Front door's open," Granger told him.

"Careless?"

"Can't be good." She had her I.D. in her left hand, right hand on her holstered pistol, as they stepped up to the door.

The bell went unanswered. Granger leaned across the threshold, calling out Walraven's name, with no result.

"Left in a hurry?" she suggested.

"Walking?" Bolan countered.

"Doubtful."

They went in with pistols drawn, cleared an expansive living room and found Walraven in the dining room. He was slumped over a table large enough for six, head turned to one side, left cheek resting in a pool of blood that had begun to drip onto the floor. Bolan made out two bullet wounds behind the right ear, scorching and grossly distorting the dead man's face, proving the shots were fired at point-blank range.

"Somebody didn't want us talking to him," Granger said.

"Or didn't want him talking period."

"You want to toss the place?"

Bolan considered it, then shook his head. "I doubt he'd bring anything incriminating to the house."

"A wasted trip then."

"Not entirely. We know someone's under pressure."

"On to Roth, then?" Granger asked.

"Sounds like a plan."

Bolan was backing out of Walraven's driveway when a throbbing sound intruded on his consciousness. Almost before it had a chance to register, he saw the helicopter rising behind the dead man's house.

"That's not Life Flight," said Granger.

No. More like the Death Flight.

"IT'S THEM, NO QUESTION," Perry Baylor said. "Stay on them."

"No problem," Kyle Warner replied.

Warner was flying the Bell 206B-3 chopper with Baylor beside him, handling the hardware. In this case, the hardware was a Minimi light machine gun produced by Fabrique Nationale d'Herstal in Belgium. Weighing in at fifteen pounds, it fed 5.56×45 mm NATO rounds from a 200-round M27 disintegrating-link belt at a cyclic rate of 700 rounds per minute. Baylor had a couple spare ammo boxes at his feet, but didn't plan on needing them.

The SUV and its two occupants were easy pickings.

No sweat.

Somebody else had taken care of Walraven before the snoops had showed up—not Baylor's business. He was paid to aim and shoot, his specialty. There was no bonus—and, in fact, could be a major penalty—for asking questions out of turn.

Now the Toyota had a jump on them, was rolling by the time their spotter had called it in, and Warner lifted off from the waste ground where they'd been sitting, waiting for their pigeons. Not that any kind of head start mattered, since the Bell's turboshaft engine gave the whirlybird a top speed of 139 miles per hour, versus the RAV4's—what? maybe 100 mph on a straightaway?

Not even close.

Some might have figured it was overkill, using the chopper for a hit that would normally call for infantry, maybe a drive-by, but another team had bitched the first attempt and had caused a shitload of embarrassment for all concerned. Not good. Today was payback, and the boss had dropped his plan of picking up the snoops alive, to question them.

He figured they were safer dead, and that was Perry Baylor's game.

He'd learned it in Iraq, found out that he enjoyed it, got a little extra practice in Afghanistan and then discovered he could make a profit from his new favorite pastime. Someone always

needed killing, and he'd learned that there was always someone willing to arrange it, if the price was right.

The SUV was rolling south on Mansfield Highway, past
Cedar Hill Memorial Park, all those dead folks underground
oblivious to what was happening around them. Coming up, the
driver had a choice of heading east on Turner Warnell Road
to catch State Highway 287, or turning west onto Dick Price
Road to make a run through open country.

Warner knew which option he was hoping for, but if he had
to chase the RAV4 down a four-lane highway, take it out in front
of several hundred witnesses, he could do that, too.

Why not?

It wouldn't be as clean a job, but hell, it wasn't like the gawkers down below would see his face.

"What's the delay?" Warner asked him, voice small and
tinny in his earphones.

"Hold your horses. I just want to see which way he's going."

"Trouble is, he's *going*. Do it, will ya?"

"Just a minute."

It was Dick Price Road, westbound, and Baylor smiled over
his gun sights, finger tightening around the Minimi's trigger.
He fired a short burst, half a dozen rounds, and wasn't surprised when he missed the Toyota. Hunting from the air took
practice and finesse. Also a pilot who could hold the chopper
steady for a nice, clean kill.

"Edge over to the left a little," he instructed Warner. "Gimme
room to work here."

"I've got power lines on that side."

"So what? You can't fly over them?"

"I thought you liked to work up close," Warner replied.

"Give me a hundred feet. I'll make 'em dance the High-
land fling."

"A hundred feet it is," said Warner, as the Bell began to climb.

"WE'RE SITTING DUCKS," said Granger.

"Running ducks," Matt Cooper corrected her. "Not sitting."

"Feels the same to me." She clutched a handgrip on the window post beside her, useless pistol in her left hand, as he swerved to dodge another burst of automatic fire. "God*damn* it! How'd he get ahead of us this time?"

"Maybe the law of averages. They couldn't *know* that we'd be coming, but they killed Walraven anyway," Cooper said.

"To shut him up?"

"Or cut deadwood. He may have done his part. Outlived his usefulness."

"Does us no good," she muttered, knowing that she sounded peevish, but to hell with that. She had a right to be pissed off, stuck in her second ambush within less than twelve hours. "We can't outrun that bird, you know."

A third burst rattled past them as she spoke, one of the slugs hitting the RAV4's low-slung luggage rack on her side, whining into space. Another inch or less, it would have pierced the roof and might have wiped out all her worries in a blinding flare of pain.

Granger wished she could at least return fire, but she didn't have an angle on the chopper, flying high and wide off to their left. Cooper whipped the SUV from side to side, swerving across both empty lanes. He was spoiling the airborne shooter's aim so far, but how good did a machine gunner really have to be? Granger hung on, expecting each moment to be her last, with a storm of slugs ripping the life out of her body, hoping that the pain was brief.

"Oh, shit!"

A farmer's pickup truck, loaded with hay bales, was pulling out in front of them, emerging from a private driveway on their right, the guy behind its wheel oblivious to what was happening around him. Had the windows up, she saw, lips moving, maybe singing with the radio or talking on a wireless headset. Either way, he nearly missed the RAV4 rushing toward him, goosed it at the final instant. Raised a bony fist as if to threaten Cooper.

That was the end of him, as bullets slashed across the pickup's windshield, turned it into pebbled safety glass and chopped the farmer's face in half. Cooper sped on by, Granger turning in her seat to watch the pickup swerve across their lane and leave the pavement, nosing down into a grassy ditch. It tilted dangerously, then stopped short of rolling over on its side.

Call it the flying shooter's error or a human sacrifice on their behalf—it hardly mattered. The farmer's death had bought them little time, if any. Granger wished the RAV4 had a sunroof she could turn into a gun port, but the wishing got her nowhere. If they didn't find some cover soon…

Ahead she saw that Dick Price Road looped northward. Trees were coming up on either side, more on the left than the right. Farmhouses were set back from the road, but if they took it off the blacktop, in among the trees, they just might have a fighting chance.

"Can you go off there, to the left?" she asked.

Cooper got it, flashed a quick smile as he tapped the brake, twisted the steering wheel and jounced across the gravel shoulder through a gap between two stately elms. A few yards farther and the woods closed in around them, overhanging branches covering the SUV. Not bulletproof, of course, but any cover was a big improvement over the open road.

As soon as Cooper had stopped and killed the RAV4's engine, Granger bailed out on her side, popping open the backdoor for a grab at Cooper's Benelli M4 Super 90 shotgun. He already had the Colt AR-15 in hand, a better weapon in their present circumstance, but Granger would make do with what she had.

The chopper made a pass, then circled back over the trees, trying to catch a glimpse of them below. This was the crunch, a gamble, since she knew they couldn't simply hide and wait it out. Somebody would be phoning for the county sheriff soon, and Granger didn't want to see him. Didn't have an explanation handy that would do the trick. Her badge might keep her out of jail, but what about Matt Cooper?

They had to take down the chopper and quickly. Which meant breaking cover.

So do it! Granger thought and made her move.

THE FIGHT COULD end in one of three ways, Bolan thought. Best case scenario, they could bring down the chopper or inflict sufficient damage on it for the pilot to turn tail and run. Worst case, the shooter in the sky could cut them down with automatic fire. Between the two extremes, police could roll up on the scene, prompting the helicopter to depart, but taking them into custody.

He liked plan A the best but wasn't sure that they could pull it off.

Tree cover worked both ways, obstructing vision from the ground as well as from the air. Bullets would pass through leafy cover, maybe sent off course by an obstructing limb, but hits came down to luck rather than skill. Bolan would have to see his target if he planned to bring it down. Which meant the target could see him.

Granger had grasped the same idea, leaving the SUV and breaking toward a clearing twenty yards away, closer to the road. Bolan could hear the chopper coming back, ready to make a strafing run, as Granger reached the open ground and lifted the Benelli's muzzle toward the sky. Maybe the first time shooting skeet had been a lethal proposition.

Bolan didn't like her chances with the twelve-gauge. The Benelli's killing range with buckshot was approximately fifty yards, at which range the double-O buckshot—nine pellets per cartridge, each one a .33-caliber missile—would scatter in a cone-shaped pattern roughly four feet in diameter. There was a chance she'd hit the chopper, probably without inflicting any major damage; much less likely that she'd tag the shooter or the pilot.

She was out there trying, though—and in the process, she was drawing fire.

Bolan reached the clearing as the helicopter thundered overhead, Granger still tracking it, still firing, as a rain of bullets stirred the soil around her, somehow missing flesh and bone, spent brass cascading from the gunship almost as an afterthought. Granger had fired half of the shotgun's eight rounds by the time Bolan arrived to chase the Bell with what turned out to be a wasted double-tap.

But it was coming back.

"Persistent little bastard," Granger said.

"He likely can't afford to go home empty-handed."

"Hope we disappoint him," she replied.

"I'm counting on it," Bolan said, the Colt AR-15 already at his shoulder.

Hunting from the air, their two-man opposition team had drawbacks of its own. The shooter couldn't alternate from one door to the other without getting in the pilot's way. That meant the chopper could not simply turn around and make another pass, returning on the same course it had followed going east to west.

The pilot had to give his gunner access from the starboard side, which meant a wider looping turn that brought the Bell back into line along the rural highway, with the clearing to its right. Five seconds, maybe ten, in wasted time. Bolan used the brief hiatus to prepare himself.

He knew the deadly math by heart: leading a target, calculating angles and velocities, allowing for assorted variables such as windage, air resistance, drag force, bullet drop, sun glare, even the beating of his heart. Bolan also knew the vulnerable aspects of a helicopter: pilot, passenger, engine, fuel tank, battery and wiring, rotors and their cables.

Inside the chopper, each projectile from his Colt would spall and tumble, causing greater damage than a straight shot through and through. But Bolan's task was still to hit a vital spot, on men or the machine, rather than simply punching holes through empty portions of the fuselage or cabin.

Do it right, and they could walk away from this. Screw up, and they could both be dead before he got a second chance.

Don't screw it up then, Bolan thought, tracking the chopper with his sights.

6

"Get closer, will you?" Perry Baylor snapped. "I still can't see a goddamned thing!"

"You know they're shooting at us, right?" Kyle Warner answered back, voice waspish in his headphones.

"Well, they *won't* be when I dust 'em. But I need a freakin' shot!"

"Awright! Awright!"

The pilot clearly didn't like it, but he did as he'd been told, making another circuit of the wooded ground below them where the SUV had disappeared, seeking an angle on the man and woman they'd been sent to kill.

Baylor was pissed off at himself, as much as anything, thinking he should have taken out the Toyota before its driver had a chance to roll it under cover. Nothing wrong with the Minimi, so it had to be his aim, or else the target's fancy driving.

Baylor didn't have to check his watch to know that they were running short on time. The kind of air show they'd been putting on would have the local yokels cranking up their antique phones and calling Sheriff Goober to the rescue any minute.

That meant Tarrant County, and he knew that the sheriff's department had a couple of Bell OH-58 Kiowa helicopters adapted from their military function to a law enforcement application. That didn't worry Baylor, since the Kiowas would have been stripped of their air-to-air fighting hardware.

Unlike Baylor's ride.

He didn't *want* to shoot down any sheriff's whirlybirds, mind you, but if they forced him to it…well, he had his orders, after all. And they did not include going to jail.

He saw a clearing down below now, and Baylor couldn't help smiling when he saw the woman waiting for him, aiming skyward with some kind of shotgun, like she thought she was duck-hunting. True Ranger spirit, but she obviously wasn't clear on how this game was played. He was beyond effective range for any twelve-gauge load and about to chop her into mincemeat, when her sidekick suddenly popped out from cover with some kind of military-looking rifle and started peppering the chopper like a pro.

Warner let out a howl as one slug pierced their windshield and another came up through the floor, between his feet. Baylor was firing back, trying to make them dance, but it was hell holding a target in his sights when Warner kept the chopper bucking like some cheap ride at a carnival.

"Goddamn it, Kyle!"

The bullet took Baylor then, a lucky shot that drilled the outside of his right thigh, as the chopper tilted toward his enemies. It came out through his inner thigh, blood spraying his pilot's clothes, and Baylor knew he was in trouble. The femoral artery, no doubt about it. Baylor had to clamp a hand there, had to stop the bleeding right away, which meant he wasn't shooting. But the sniper on the ground kept firing up at them nonstop.

Now there was smoke inside the helicopter's cabin, blurring Baylor's vision, choking him. Warner was cursing, fighting the controls and getting nowhere, as the chopper pitched and yawed across green treetops, out over a stretch of desert to the west.

"I need to set it down!" the pilot shouted, deafening through his earphones.

Baylor knew he should ask Kyle how in hell they were supposed to get away without their bird, but Baylor was too dry mouthed to speak. Funny, because all around him, including his trousers, boots and the floorboard beneath him were awash in blood. He tried to hold the Minimi one-handed, his fingers weak and slippery, but couldn't manage it. What did it matter, anyhow, since he had missed his shot?

Warner was grappling with the cyclic stick and the collective lever, dancing on the antitorque pedals, about as useful as if he'd been strumming on a ukulele. They were spinning now and seemed to be accelerating at the same time, as if they'd been sucked into a tornado Baylor couldn't see. They damned sure weren't in Kansas anymore, and from the blurred landscape in front of him, he couldn't swear that it was Texas, either.

More like hell, in fact.

He couldn't read the chopper's gauges, but who needed an altimeter to tell him that they were in a nosedive, headed for the desert at a hundred miles an hour, maybe faster? In his fantasies, Baylor had always thought that, when his time came, he'd have something cool to say. Now it had caught him by surprise.

There wasn't even time to scream.

The helicopter blew on impact, its ruptured fuel tank spilling fire. The rotor blades snapped off and skittered off across the flatland, clipping sage and desert willows. Oily smoke rose straight up for a hundred feet or so, then caught a breeze and fled eastward in tatters, staining the pale blue sky.

"You hit?" asked Bolan.

"No," said Granger. "You?"

"I'm fine."

"I think he dinged your ride a time or two."

"Cosmetics," Bolan said. "We need to clear out while we can."

He couldn't quote an average response time for the local law and didn't want to test it. Someone must have placed a call by now, unless the nearby farmhouses were all deserted. Even then there was no reason to remain and press their luck.

The RAV4 featured permanent all-wheel drive, nothing to shift or fiddle with on the dashboard as Bolan gunned it around through a U-turn and out of the grove that had saved them from being shot to pieces moments earlier. Back on the road, he put a hasty mile behind them, then slowed down to an approximation of the posted speed limit, not racing like a fugitive or creeping like a driver with a snoot full, trying to avoid a DUI stop.

Normal, right, after a running firefight with a helicopter, twenty miles or less from downtown Dallas.

And Big D was their destination, although at the moment they were headed west, away from it and toward Fort Worth. The plan was fairly simple: catch West Pioneer Parkway to West Loop 820 northbound, then pick up Interstate 30—also known as the Tom Landry Freeway, named for the late Dallas Cowboys coach—eastbound, back into Dallas.

Looking for a rocket man.

"You think we'll get to him in time?" asked Granger.

Him was George Roth, head of Lone Star Aerospace's program, a NASA castoff who had found a new home and had greatly increased his annual salary by signing up with Lamar Ridgway's team.

"No way to tell," Bolan replied. "What do you know about him?"

"He's got rockets in his blood," said Granger. "Third generation German immigrant. His granddad was one of the whiz kids our government picked up from Adolf's gang after World War II, along with von Braun and that bunch."

"Operation Paperclip?"

"Whatever. His grandfather's name was Herman Rothmann when he got here with his wife and kids, but someone trimmed it down to Roth. The son—that's Frederick—picked up his Ph.D. from Stanford and went on the NASA payroll, working at their Jet Propulsion Laboratory while his daddy helped put Alan Shepard into orbit. Grandson Georgie got his doctorate at Rensselaer Polytechnic Institute and joined the team in time to do his bit for the space shuttle program and the International Space Station before austerity kicked in."

"You've done your homework," Bolan said.

"I was a Girl Scout. 'Be prepared,' you know?"

"It rings a bell."

"So I've been wondering. I know it sounds far-fetched, but

what if Roth had something more than fascination with the universe passed down to him from Grandpa and his dad?"

"Ex-Nazis," Bolan said.

"You think they're ever really *ex?*"

"Depends," he said, "if they were true believers or got forced into the party for survival's sake."

"Maybe. But if you heard the old war stories growing up, the blitz and V-2 rockets smashing into London, rockets that your grandpa built, it might sink in."

"Something to ask him, anyway," Bolan agreed.

"Assuming that we get the chance."

Walraven's execution bothered Bolan, only for the loss of a potential source. If George Roth was the next to go, they might be robbed of any chance to look inside the Ridgway operation, short of a direct assault, and he preferred to gain more detailed information prior to using that approach.

But he would take what he could get and run with it.

That was the way a warrior rolled.

Forest Hills, Dallas

GEORGE ROTH WAS not accustomed to a sense of panic, and he hated it. The call had come as he was sitting down to breakfast; Simon Coetzee on the line, advising him of a security breach at Lone Star Aerospace Technology. When Roth had asked the nature of that breach, he'd been informed that there was no time for discussion. He must simply pack "a few things for the road" and be prepared to leave his home within the next half hour.

A few things for the road?

How could he choose among his favorite suits—the Fioravanti, the Enzo D'Orsi, the Armani? Never mind his shirts and sweaters, what about his Prada shoes, his Berluti footwear? *Gott im Himmel,* how could he walk off and leave his home?

Forest Hills, south of White Rock Lake in east Dallas, features many grand homes, and Roth's estate, on Garland Road, was one of them. Not a palace, of course, only thirty-five rooms. But with the touches he had added since he had bought it, after joining Lone Star Aerospace Technology, it was the very home he'd dreamed of all his life. More perfect still because he lived in it alone. And now to leave it like a thief surprised while looting in the middle of the night…

Unthinkable. But Coetzee offered him no alternative.

The move was temporary, he'd been told. And for his own protection, naturally. When could he return? Coetzee had no idea just now, but Roth's safety was foremost on the Big Man's mind.

Lamar Ridgway, that is.

The nickname evidently sprang from the size of his bankroll, since Ridgway himself was below-average height, at five foot six. Roth managed not to laugh when people used the silly sobriquet in front of him, since Ridgway paid Roth's very handsome salary and treated him with absolute respect whenever they were drawn together at the plant Roth supervised.

Until today.

Being uprooted from his home, his *life,* was not respectful. Trying to imagine what grave danger could precipitate such action was the cause of Roth's unprecedented panic.

He was packing, but it wasn't easy. His supremely organized and regimented mind refused to function normally under this sudden stress, so different from any challenge in a factory or laboratory where his expertise and education made him the superior of any other person in the room. This situation was unique.

And he was terrified.

Roth had barely filled one of his six Balenciaga suitcases, suddenly realizing that he'd packed no toiletries, when he was startled by the doorbell's chime. A quick glance at his Tag Heuer Aquaracer watch told Roth that only eighteen minutes had elapsed since Coetzee's warning call. He had been promised half an hour, and he wasn't ready yet!

But then he thought, what if it isn't Coetzee?

If there was a problem with security, who else might be appearing uninvited at his door?

From the top drawer of his nightstand, Roth retrieved a Walther PPS—the *Polizei-Pistole Schmal,* or Police Pistol Slim, in English—loaded with seven rounds of .40 S&W hollowpoint ammunition. With its external integrated trigger safety, the compact weapon was ready to fire, and Roth was pleased to feel no tremor in his hand as he left his bedroom, moving swiftly toward the front door of his home.

He checked the peephole first and recognized the two men standing on his doorstep. Coetzee was not present, but these two were his habitual companions when he visited the Lone Star plant.

"You're early. I was given thirty minutes."

"Time's up, Doctor," one of them replied, eyes taking in the pistol Roth held at his side. "We have a situation."

"And that is?"

"We'll talk about it in the car, Doctor," the other said. "No time to waste."

"I have a bag."

"Which way?" the first one asked.

Of course these two had never been inside his home before. Roth stood aside, directing them, not showing them his back. He kept the Walther in his hand as they proceeded toward the master bedroom.

"I still need to collect a few things," he said.

"We'll pick up whatever else you need," one of them said. "The main thing, Doctor, is to get you out of here while there's still time."

Roth didn't like the sound of that, didn't like any of this hasty business, but he had no choice in the matter. Arguing with Simon Coetzee was a waste of time on matters of security. And truth be told, despite the strain of arrogance that Roth acknowledged in himself—which had throughout his life prevented him from making any long-term friends—one thing that he did not possess was courage in the face of danger.

He would let the professionals take all the risks.

But he would keep his Walther handy, just in case.

BOLAN APPROACHED FOREST HILLS on Interstate 30, taking off on East Grand Avenue toward White Rock Lake. At the south end of the lake, East Grand turned into Garland Road, facing the water and, within three blocks, the Dallas Arboretum. He could almost smell the money there, hiding behind the tall, stately facades of English Tudor homes erected in the 1920s, when the lake—initially the city's first reservoir—had been transformed into a park and recreation area.

But Bolan had not come for relaxation. He was hunting and knew the address of his prey.

George Roth lived in a two-story house midway between St. Francis Avenue and Whittier, with no view of the lake from his front porch, but he'd still come a long way from the days when Grandpa Herman made the jump from Nazi Germany, courtesy of Operation Paperclip and the wartime Office of Strategic Services. Times change, and the OSS had folded in 1945, reborn two years later as the Central Intelligence Agency. Operation Paperclip meanwhile had morphed into Operation Lusty—for *Lu*ftwaffe *S*ecret *T*echnolog*y*—later absorbed into the National Aeronautics and Space Administration.

Magic.

Some seven hundred scientists who'd been devoted to *Der Führer* were "rehabilitated" overnight, their talents turned at first toward America's Cold War arms race against the Soviet Union, then to exploration of outer space. Today those few Americans who realized the program had existed in the first place knew it chiefly from its fictional portrayal on *The X-Files*.

Art incorporating life and grisly death.

Bolan spotted the street number Granger had given him. There was no car in the driveway, but he couldn't see beyond the closed doors of the two-car garage. Bolan parked his RAV4 at an angle in the driveway, cutting off escape by way of Garland Road, and walked up to the porch with Granger at his side.

No answer to the doorbell or his knocking. Trees screened Roth's front door from any view by neighbors to the north or south. He saw nobody stirring on the arboretum's thickly wooded grounds across the street. Bolan took a SouthOrd E500XT electric lock pick from his pocket, applied it to the front door's lock and opened it within seconds.

Silence greeted them inside Roth's home. With pistols drawn, Bolan and Granger started checking out the place, beginning on the ground floor, feeling mixed relief and disappointment as they cleared each empty room. Upstairs the process was repeated, nothing but an open closet in the master bedroom seeming out of place, given Roth's obsessive tidiness. No corpse, no bloodstains, nothing to suggest intrusion by unwanted visitors besides themselves.

"Looks like he split," said Granger.

"Wearing three suits, if the empty hangers count for anything," Bolan observed.

"Maybe he sent some to the cleaners?"

"One way to tell."

They doubled back to check out the garage. Using the entry from Roth's kitchen, Bolan found a silver Ford Explorer parked next to a black Jaguar XKR-S.

"I doubt he'd walk to work," said Granger, from the doorway just behind him.

"Doesn't look like he'd be in the market for a taxi, either," Bolan said.

"Carpooling?"

"I'd bet on evacuation."

"Damn it! Now what?"

"When all else fails," Bolan replied, "we turn the game around."

"Meaning?"

"Instead of chasing them, let them catch us."

"Can't say I like the sound of that too much."

"I'll break it down," he told her, "on the way."

"To where?"

"Your place."

Preston Hollow, Dallas

"So he's good now?"

"Safe and sound, sir."

"Make damn sure you keep him that way, Simon," Ridgway ordered.

"Yes, sir. Not a problem," Coetzee promised.

"More than just your job is ridin' on that egghead."

"Understood, sir."

Ridgway cut the link without another word. He trusted Coetzee, the man he'd picked from fifty-some-odd candidates to head Lone Star's security when it became apparent that establishing a private army was the way to go. Coetzee came highly recommended and had proven himself in other crisis situations, although none as pressing as the one confronting them today.

Prowling the study of his thirty-million-dollar home, Ridgway sipped from a tumbler of vintage reserve Jameson whiskey, listed at three hundred dollars per bottle. Its touch of creamy dairy fudge and dark chocolate made Ridgway feel like he was drinking candy with a kick that went straight to his head.

Only the best for the Big Man, and why the hell not? Hadn't he clawed his way up from nothing—*less* than nothing—to stand astride his chosen world? Who else could rival him, much less stand in his way, when he was getting ready to remake that world?

Ridgway lived in Preston Hollow for the simple reason that he could. It was the most expensive neighborhood in Dallas, past and present home to celebrities including Ross Perot, George W. Bush, Mary Kay Ash, golfer Lee Trevino, British rock star George Michael, plus owners and top-ranking players of the Dallas Cowboys, Mavericks and Stars. Ridgway knew all of them by sight and socialized with none of them.

Why should he? What good was an ex-president, anyhow?

Particularly when he had a future president in his hip pocket and a brand-new country to go with him?

All he had to do was keep the damned thing from unraveling around him as they got down to the wire. Some pissant Texas Ranger figured she could pull the plug on Ridgway's grand design? She'd better think again and maybe run for cover while her brains were still inside her skull. He just might let her live, if she found someplace nice and far away to hide—maybe the Outer Hebrides or Madagascar—and if she kept her damned mouth shut.

But, then again, he'd never have a guarantee of that, would he? Unless he put her in the ground.

Or Simon Coetzee did it for him.

And this guy who'd blown in out of nowhere, teamed up with the Ranger, leaving four dead men in San Antonio, now two more and a chopper shot to hell outside of Arlington. What kind of crazy shit was that?

Ridgway would definitely love to meet *that* guy, find out who he was working for, but something told Ridgway that it wasn't in the cards. He knew hard-chargers when he saw them, had destroyed some in his time and had hired some others to do their hard-charging for him. There was a world of difference between the *real* tough guys and those who hung around on street corners, half in the bag by noon and spoiling for a confrontation with some milquetoast SOB they could push around.

No, Ridgway doubted very much that he would ever have a chance to speak with Texas Ranger Adlene Granger's new imported sidekick. But he planned to crush the nervy bastard pretty goddamn soon, before he tossed a monkey wrench into the works and ruined everything.

The men who'd founded Texas in the first place weren't afraid of General Antonio López de Santa Anna at the Alamo, or later, when they'd kicked his ragged ass at San Jacinto. Ridgway, born of sturdy Texas stock himself, had yet to meet an adversary whom he couldn't buy, beat down, burn out or otherwise eliminate.

This was his game. He made the rules.

As for the rest of what had once been a united country standing tall and proud, the pompous asses who imagined they were in control would never know what hit them.

7

Johnson County, Texas

Rolling south from Dallas on I-35, Bolan asked Granger, "How long have you lived in Waco?"

"Coming up on eighteen months," she said. "Company F covers thirty-eight counties, from Hill down to Atascosa, and across to Calhoun on the Gulf."

"How many Rangers in the company?"

"Twenty-five, including one major and three lieutenants." She shifted gears and asked, "You want to tell me what we're doing now? The last I heard, you thought Lone Star or Crockett's boys would have my place staked out."

"I'm betting on it," Bolan said.

"So…what? We walk into the trap?"

"I'd prefer to turn it around," he replied. "Ideally pick up one of them and have a little heart-to-heart about whatever Ridgway and the NTR have planned."

"Okay. Let's say we bag one and he won't talk. Then what?"

Bolan met the Ranger's gaze and told her, "I'm not taking any prisoners."

She lapsed back into silence while he pushed the RAV4 on toward Waco, eighty-odd miles south of Dallas, in McLennan County. A midsized city of some 125,000 inhabitants, nearly leveled by a catastrophic tornado in 1953, still edgy about the tragic ATF/FBI siege forty years later. Granger's home, she'd told him, was a five-room apartment downtown, a short walk from Dr Pepper Museum on South Fifth Street.

Not the best place for a firefight, granted, but he hoped they could avoid one. And if not…well, he had managed worse, in vastly larger and more crowded cities nationwide. Around the world, in fact.

"So, what's the plan?" Granger inquired, as they entered Hill County from the north. "You have a plan, right?"

"More or less," Bolan agreed.

"Not sure I like the sound of that."

"How's this—whoever has your place staked out, assuming that it *is* staked out, they won't know me by sight. Whether they're with Lone Star or Crockett's gang, no one who's seen me so far has had time to carry tales."

"Agreed."

Six dead and counting on the other side.

"Even if they've been told to take you down on sight," he said, "they'll have to wonder who I am, if I show up and let myself inside."

"Alone?" she asked.

"As far as they can see."

"And then?"

"I'm guessing that they'll want to pick me up and have a chat. At least see who I am, find out if I can tell them where to find you."

"So they follow you inside?"

"Ideally," Bolan said.

"And where am I, while this is going on?"

"Close by. Ready to close the trap."

"In my apartment."

"Either that, or on the street."

"That's not much of a choice."

"Plan B is going after Crockett and his people at their compound, which will have to wait for nightfall."

"And plan C?" she asked.

"Ridgway."

"No. We should have a better grip on what they're planning first, before we tackle either one of those."

He nodded. "Your place then?"

"You sure know how to charm a girl."

Hill County had a population roughly one-third the size of Waco's, with one-quarter of its people residing at the county seat of Hillsboro. Most of its 960 square miles were given over to sparse desert growth, some trees standing guard over I-35 as it carried them southward. The landscape made Bolan think of outlaws, rattlesnakes and Western movies he'd enjoyed in childhood, where the good guys always won.

Not like the real world he inhabited.

In that world, bad guys often prospered and enjoyed their wealth with no real threat of punishment for their crimes. Government collusion often smoothed the way, and even when convictions were obtained—or when the Executioner stepped in to settle matters out of court—no victory for the good guys was ever permanent. Remove one predator, or a hundred, and there were always more to fill the void, eager for their promotion to the big time.

"You think we'll have to trash my place?" Granger inquired.

"It could become a crime scene."

"Marvelous."

"In which case, what becomes of your bereavement leave?"

"Good question," she replied, sounding glum. "I guess we'll have to wait and see."

Preston Hollow, Dallas

MALCOLM BARNHART LOVED the smell of money. Not the grubby scent of currency that passed from hand to hand, but rather the rarefied atmosphere of affluence and power that surrounded people with money to burn. An odd expression, when he thought about it, since the last thing he would ever do with cash was set it on fire.

Spend it, certainly, with circumspection, to avoid a conflict with the tax man. Bank it in the Caymans, the Bahamas, Switzerland, wherever fortunes were secure from prying eyes and auditors. Use it to get exactly what he wanted—which was more of everything.

Particularly influence.

Barnhart had grown up in the murky world of Texas politics, watching his father run for governor time and again, never progressing any further than the state House of Representatives, where he'd filled a seat from Bastrop County for a single two-year term. It had been Barnhart's lifelong dream to pick up where his old man had left off, go all the way to Austin, maybe even on to Washington someday.

But until recently he'd never thought that he might be president.

Now that had changed.

Not president of the United States. That was a fantasy—and who would want the job today, the way once-proud America had gone to hell? No, Barnhart had a shot at something better, something realistically attainable, in his opinion.

And the trick was not to screw it up.

The phone call from Lamar Ridgway had been a summons, plain and simple. When the oil man told Barnhart to jump, Barnhart replied, "How high?" Sometimes, just for good measure, he might add, "How many times?"

He never had to ask, "Which way?" Lamar inevitably spelled that out in simple English, telling Barnhart what to do and how it should be done. Sometimes he had a script prepared for Barnhart. And when it came to thinking, Barnhart did his level best to see the world through Ridgway's eyes.

He harbored no illusions about being independent, holding power in his own right, making any of the big decisions on his own. It was a game of strategy, played out on levels he had barely glimpsed from Bastrop County and for stakes that still bewildered him. He was content to be a pampered pawn.

For now, at least.

Ridgway's butler greeted Barnhart with a nod and took his

Stetson, hung it on a hat rack that they passed en route to Ridgway's study. When the butler knocked, Ridgway's familiar voice growled, "Enter!"

"Mr. Barnhart here to see you, sir."

"Malcolm, come in! Come in!"

Ridgway was standing near the wet bar, topping off a glass of Jameson's—the only thing Barnhart had ever seen him drink, besides iced tea. Based on the color in his cheeks, Barnhart surmised that Ridgway had been drinking through the morning, but with his epic capacity for alcohol, it scarcely seemed to matter. He was clear-eyed and alert, as always.

"Drink?"

"I wouldn't mind a cold Corona," Barnhart said.

"We've got 'em. Help yourself."

Barnhart retrieved a longneck and uncapped it, didn't bother with a glass or slice of lime. "You mentioned something on the phone about a problem, sir."

"Maybe I should've said a challenge. Are you ready to proceed if we advance the schedule?"

Barnhart felt a tingle of excitement laced with apprehension, unrelated to the ice-cold beer. "Advance?" he parroted.

"To later in the week."

"*This* week?"

"Maybe tomorrow or the next day," Ridgway said.

"Well, um…I mean…it was supposed to be—"

"Next month, I know. Something's come up."

"If I may ask…"

"No need to dwell on details," Ridgway said. "I'm handling it, but there's a chance something could leak ahead of time. So are you ready?"

Any further hesitation could be fatal. "Yes, sir," Barnhart answered. "Absolutely!"

"Good. We're this close—" Ridgway raised his free hand, thumb and index finger half an inch apart "—from being ready with the big punch, just in case the *federales* try to shut us down. Once that's ready to go, I'd say tomorrow at the latest, we'll announce it and watch the bastards run around like headless chickens."

Barnhart forced a smile, then sipped his beer. It tasted flat now, even though he heard it fizzing in the bottle.

Christ, tomorrow! He'd been marking days off on the calendar, anticipation mounting, but to lose a month of preparation time…

To hell with it. Barnhart reckoned he was as ready as he'd ever be.

To lead a brand-new nation, sure. Why not?

Rivercrest, Fort Worth, Texas

"AND HOW LONG must I stay here?"

Simon Coetzee watched George Roth pacing around the mansion's library, hands stuffed into his trouser pockets to keep them from twitching nervously. "We're not sure yet. As long as necessary," he replied.

"I have important work to do," Roth said. His voice was nearly childlike in its petulance.

"You'll be transported to the plant later this morning."

"And tonight?"

"Back here," said Coetzee. "Under guard."

"If I'm to be a prisoner, you could be guarding me at home."

"First, you are not a prisoner. We are protecting you from harm. And second, we must take for granted that the enemy knows where you live."

"These enemies," Roth said, turning to face Coetzee. "Who are they?"

"That remains to be determined. Mr. Ridgway will explain to you in due time, I am sure."

"But if you don't know who they are—"

"There have been incidents." Time for a little shock and awe. "Craig Walraven is dead."

"Walraven! How?"

"Shot in his home," Coetzee replied. No reason to explain that he had carried out that execution on the Big Man's orders.

"My God! But—"

"Now you see why you could not remain in Dallas and pursue your normal schedule. No one knows about this house. They cannot find you here."

"Can you be sure of that?"

"I'm certain."

The safe house Roth and Coetzee occupied was in Rivercrest, one of Fort Worth's most desirable neighborhoods. Located on Tremont Avenue, the house had been built for a Confederate general, then renovated in the 1920s for a new generation of wealthy Texans. It was owned by a subsidiary of Lone Star Petroleum, with no reference to L. E. Ridgway on the deed.

Untraceable.

"And is the plant secure?" Roth asked.

"No worries there."

Coetzee had thrown a ring of men with guns around the place, doubling the normal guard, which was substantial in the first place. Nothing, no one, would be permitted to derail the Big Man's plan.

"Can you eliminate this danger?" Roth inquired.

"It's being handled." Not so well, thus far, but why upset the genius?

"Good. I wouldn't want to live here for a month."

"No problem." Coetzee sipped his coffee, wishing it was a bottle of Castle Lager. And again, there was no need to tell Roth that the schedule had been drastically advanced. Let the Big Man break it to him in his own inimitable style.

"I ought to have a weapon," Roth declared. "For self-defense."

"Protecting you is my job," Coetzee said.

"As you protected Walraven?"

Touché.

"Are you experienced with firearms?"

"From my childhood," Roth replied. "My grandfather, as you may know, was in the military."

More specifically, an *oberst,* or colonel, in the Allgemeine SS, assigned to the V-2 rocket works at Peenemünde, on Germany's Baltic coast. The closest he had ever come to battle was the day he had surrendered to U.S. forces in June of 1945.

"I may be able to provide you with a pistol," Coetzee said. "You have a preference, from personal experience?"

"Nine millimeter," Roth replied. "Perhaps a Walther or Beretta?"

"That should not be difficult." He had an arsenal at his disposal; pistols were the least of it. "I'll have a sampling waiting for you when you leave the plant today."

"Thank you." The words were stiff, as if Roth found it difficult to speak them.

He was certainly a prick, as Coetzee had decided on the day they had met. Roth's background—his familial history, the inbred arrogance—made simple courtesy unnatural, even distasteful to him, though he managed to perform within the standards of so-called polite society. Coetzee had known men of his type, back in South Africa, diehards from the old National Party, now mostly affiliated with the separatist Afrikaner Volksfront. They were living in the past.

Unlike the Big Man, who had laid the groundwork for a revolutionary future.

Now all that remained was to fire the opening shot.

Tom Green County

"MISSED 'EM AGAIN, by God!" said Waylon Crockett. "Fancy plan fell through. They shoulda let us do the job ourselves."

Kent Luttrell sipped from a mason jar of clear corn whiskey, savoring the burn, and passed it off to Crockett. He was not about to mention how their own men had screwed up the first attempt to bag their enemies.

"That Cozy fella works for Ridgway," Crockett groused, garbling Coetzee's name. "He ain't even American."

"Can't argue with the Big Man," said Luttrell, glancing around in case someone was listening.

And then felt foolish for it. They were walking near the fence line of the compound, buildings clustered to the west of them, nearly a quarter mile away. Nothing but cactus, creosote and lizards on this portion of the property, maybe a red-tailed hawk from time to time. Luttrell's men drove around outside the compound twice a day, checking for Feds or sheriff's deputies who might be lying in the weeds with parabolic microphones or some such gear to eavesdrop, and they'd found nothing so far.

That didn't rule out drones or satellite surveillance, but Luttrell didn't concern himself too much with that. The CIA or NSA could read a name tag on your shirt from outer space, all right, but sound was out. As far as spying from the sky went, he had drilled the compound's residents to keep their more exotic weapons under cover when they left the buildings. Ammo and explosives, with the big guns, moved through tunnels excavated underneath the desert settlement, hidden from flying eyes.

"They're movin' up the deadline," Crockett said, after a shot of whiskey oiled his tongue and calmed his nerves a bit. "Good thing, I say."

"Uh-huh."

Luttrell agreed in principle, of course, but it was also worrisome. It made things *real*. They weren't just playing soldier anymore, talking about a revolution that could happen next year or five years from now. There'd been no urgency to speak of in the planning stages. Even when they'd hooked up with the Big Man, it still sounded like a fantasy. Like playacting. Now folks had started dying, and The Day had been advanced. The rhetoric was giving way to action, and Luttrell would have been lying if he'd said it didn't scare him, just a little.

The way it all had been explained to him, it sounded like a breeze. Secession, backed up by the big surprise that Mr. Ridgway had planned out, and nothing Washington could do about it without starting World War III right in their own backyard. The more he thought about it, though, the more it sounded just a mite *too* simple.

Would the president really take it lying down? Or would he send the army, air force, navy and marines to kick ass all the way from Corpus Christi to the Texas Panhandle? Luttrell knew there were fourteen active U.S. military bases in the state, ready for action when the order came, but would they risk it after Ridgway showed his hole card?

No way to tell, until that hand was dealt and played.

One thing Luttrell had promised to himself: no matter how it finally went down, he'd never see the inside of a prison cell. *Live free or die,* and hadn't Adolf shown the way? He could've wimped out and surrendered to the Russkies back in '45, instead of choosing death by his own hand. Long gone but not forgotten.

When his own time came, Luttrell did not intend to make it easy for his enemies. No cyanide or pistol in the mouth. He'd go down fighting, take as many of the bastards with him as he could before they finished him. The kind of death white-power bands would sing about for years to come.

Or maybe they'd get lucky. Hell, maybe they'd actually win.

Crockett passed back the mason jar, and Kent put down another healthy swallow of the liquid fire, a product of the compound's own distillery. Another way they thumbed their noses at the Feds, just for the hell of it.

A few more days, and none of it would matter.

One way or another, it would be a whole new world.

McLennan County, Texas

MORE DESERT AS Bolan and Granger crossed the county line, with cultivated acreage here and there along I-35. The bleak landscape, to Bolan's mind, reflected both the region's history and hard times in the present day. For decades prior to World

War II, McLennan County had been known for lynchings and for public demonstrations by the Ku Klux Klan.

McLennan's most famous event, before the Waco siege, dated back to September 1896, when forty thousand spectators paid two dollars per head to watch a pair of locomotives crash head-on, deliberately, in Crush—a town established purely for this publicity stunt. Although the gawkers were supposed to be kept well back from the railroad tracks, three died in the resulting blast of ruptured boilers.

Things were quieter around McLennan County, these days, but an estimated one in five inhabitants lived below the federal poverty line.

"You get a lot of agitation here?" asked Bolan, as they passed through West, a wide spot in the road some twenty miles due north of Waco.

"Not so much," Granger replied. "A lot of people hate the government, but if you ask them why, it all comes out confused. Plenty of monthly checks go out from Medicare, social security, but people cashing them still seem to think they've got no ties to Washington. They think somebody's coming any day, to confiscate their guns or close their churches, make them swear allegiance to Sharia law. It's weird."

"Impressed by demagogues?"

"Lots of them definitely drank the snake oil," Granger said.

"Frustration does that."

"Not to mention ignorance. You may have heard that we aren't doing as well as we could be in terms of kids finishing high school. And we're something like thirtieth in bachelor's degrees, and thirty-third in graduate degrees."

"There's always common sense," Bolan replied.

"You'd think so. But what does it tell you when over two hundred thousand people believe they can just pull up stakes and start a new country?"

"Right now I'm only thinking of the ones who actually mean to try it."

"Focus, sure. I get it," Granger said.

"First pass by your apartment," Bolan advised. "You ought to stay down out of sight. I'll cruise around the block and try to pick out any watchers."

"What if they're already hiding out inside?" she asked.

"They'll be in for a rude surprise."

"Or you will."

"Chances are they won't start shooting right away," he said, "if you're not with me."

"Way to make a girl feel welcome."

"If they're *not* inside, they'll spot me going in and follow up," Bolan continued.

"Then I get to surprise them," Granger said. "I know the drill."

"We'll try to keep it quiet, for the neighbors' sake," Bolan added. "But it all depends on how the opposition wants to play it."

"I guess it makes a difference whether they're Lone Star or the NTR. That chopper wasn't Crockett's, I can tell you."

"Someone should be working on the registration," Bolan said.

"Likely the FAA, out of Fort Worth," Granger replied.

"Could be a headache for the Lone Star team."

"I doubt they'd field a chopper that was traceable to Ridgway or the company. Coetzee's smarter than that."

"Smart enough to take Walraven off the table."

"So to speak."

"And stash Roth somewhere safe."

"I would've liked to put him through the ringer," Granger said.

"We still might have a shot at him."

"You mean, if we can bag someone who knows where Coetzee's hiding him."

"With any luck."

"We need to hope it's Lone Star sitting on my place, instead of Crockett's people then. I doubt they'd share that kind of information with the NTR."

Something was nagging at the back of Bolan's mind and making him uneasy. It was one thing for a billionaire to dream of privatizing outer space. Twenty-odd American, European and Japanese firms had hatched similar plans, some busting out, with others still in various stages of development and testing. It was a different story entirely, though, if that same billionaire was a known political extremist with ready access to fissile material.

Rockets plus nukes equaled potential for disaster, maybe on a global scale.

For all he knew, the countdown clock was running, even now.

And if they couldn't find the rocket man, how would they shut it down?

8

Waco, Texas

"How long are we supposed to wait around out here?" Ben Godwin asked.

"Long as it takes," Roy Mattox answered. "You got someplace else to be?"

"I'd like to wrap it up, is all," Godwin replied.

"We do the job Simon assigned to us," Mattox reminded him. "Nobody said we have to like it."

They'd been sitting in the Jeep Grand Cherokee, outside a Stripes store on Clay Avenue, since six o'clock that morning. Mattox had arranged it with the manager, showed him a set of bogus FBI credentials and explained about their classified surveillance job, a matter of security and yada, yada, so the guy wouldn't get nervous and dime them out to Waco P.D. They were feeding the kitty besides, with their coffee and sodas and snacks, all of it going onto Lone Star's tab.

A block north of the store, they had a clear view of their target. It was an apartment house, six units, one of them belonging to the Texas Ranger they were waiting for. She hadn't turned up yet, but until she did, the four of them were under orders to remain on station, ready to move in the moment she showed.

"We oughta rotate," Colin Page suggested, from his backseat vantage point. "Get Otto out of there and let somebody else relax a while."

"Otto's on duty, same as you," said Mattox.

Godwin snorted. "Likely going through her underwear right now."

The fourth member of their surveillance team was Otto Franks. He'd drawn the short straw when they'd picked a man to stake out the apartment from inside. The locks were nothing special, barely took a minute, and he would be waiting for the Ranger, if and when she finally came home. Surprise her and attempt to chill her out while Mattox and the others rolled in for support.

And if she gave him any trouble, put her down.

That was the latest word from Simon Coetzee since two prior attempts had failed to bag the Ranger and some guy she'd picked up in San Antonio, an unknown quantity who'd done his share of ass-kicking since midnight. There were big things happening, important things, and now these wild cards had come along, trying to screw it up. Coetzee had wanted them alive, for questioning, but after two snafus on that end, he had changed the game plan.

The Ranger and her boyfriend were no longer wanted dead or alive.

Just dead.

That made it easier for Mattox and his crew, although a hit in downtown Waco still required a certain measure of finesse. Police headquarters was only nine blocks away, on North Fourth Street, so they couldn't afford any kind of Wild West shoot-'em-up action. All four carried silencer-equipped semiautomatic pistols, and Colin had a Heckler & Koch MP5SD6 in the backseat, also fitted with a factory-standard sound suppressor, in case they needed heavier firepower.

Mattox hoped it wouldn't come to that. He figured if they had to use the submachine gun, it meant something had gone wrong. Four trained professionals should have no problem taking down a hick cop and her pal without a major firefight in the street.

He hoped.

Simon was running out of patience, with the Big Man riding

him, and neither of them would look kindly on another failure. Not that it would matter, since the last six guys who'd washed out on the job were dead.

Something to think about.

They couldn't take the Ranger and her pal for granted as a pair of easy marks. Even discounting Crockett's rednecks on the first attempt, Mattox had known the boys who had blown up in Arlington as tried-and-true professionals. And they'd been *airborne*—believe it or not—but they'd fumbled the job all the same.

Not this time.

Mattox knew his life and reputation were riding on this job, and he planned to do it right.

"Who's this?" asked Godwin, from the driver's seat.

A tall man coming toward the target address, walking south along Clay Avenue. He stopped in front of the apartment house, passed through its little open gate and went up to the porch.

"Could be the sidekick," Page suggested, though they had no physical description of the man.

"Otto will take him, if it is," said Mattox.

"No sign of the cop."

"Not yet," Mattox agreed. "Just keep your eyes peeled and be ready when I give the word."

BOLAN HAD MADE one pass along Clay Avenue, not wanting to be obvious, with Granger lying out of sight in the RAV4's backseat. He made the three guys in the Jeep Grand Cherokee, relieved to note the SUV's civilian license plate. They weren't lawmen. When they tried to close the trap, Bolan could use whatever force he thought was necessary, with no worries about violating any aspect of his private code.

Three men. But were they on their own?

He spotted no more lookouts on the street, no other pairs or individuals idling suspiciously in cars parked at the curb. There was a possibility of watchers in some residence along Clay Avenue—impossible to check out unless he started going door to door. Ridiculous. If *he* were setting up the trap, Bolan supposed he would try to get inside Granger's apartment, or at least one of the others in her building, where he'd have quick access if she showed.

He drove around the block and parked on Webster Avenue, just down from the Fort House Museum. "Give me a minute," he told Granger, still concealed, "then switch up to the driver's seat. I'll keep in touch remotely as I go."

"Okay," she said, invisible to Bolan in the SUV's rearview.

They'd picked up a pair of Cobra CXR925 walkie-talkies with a thirty-five-mile range, plus two Cobra GA-EBM2 ear-buds with compact microphones that left hands free for other business in a crunch. The walkies featured twenty-two channels and 142 privacy codes, and a digital voice recorder, just in case one of them missed a message in the heat of action. As it was, they'd have no trouble maintaining contact over two blocks in the heart of downtown Waco.

Leaving the Toyota, Bolan reversed direction and walked against one-way traffic on South Fourth Street, then turned right, heading southwestward, on Clay Avenue. Down range, he saw the Stripes store and the Jeep Grand Cherokee, ignoring both as he moved on toward Granger's home address, at midblock on his right.

She'd sketched the layout for him, and he had committed it to memory, palming the key to her front door. No one appeared to notice Bolan as he turned in through the open knee-high gate between the sidewalk and a small but neatly tended lawn. He climbed three concrete steps, passed through the front door that was left unlocked during daylight hours, as Granger had informed him. Past a bank of six mailboxes, up a flight of stairs to reach the second floor, key in his left hand, right hand ready for a dive inside his open jacket if he had to reach one of the Glocks.

"I'm in," he said into the walkie-talkie.

"Copy that," Granger replied, her voice small in his ear.

The stairs creaked slightly under Bolan's weight, an older

house making its normal sounds. No one had tried to intercept him on the ground floor, and he took his time ascending
to the second-story landing. Once there Bolan paused and listened, heard nothing, assumed the other tenants were off at
their daily jobs.

In fact the place was quiet as a tomb.

"Upstairs now," Bolan said.

No answer from the earpiece, but he pictured Granger at
the RAV4's wheel, biding her time. He moved along the hallway to his left, one door on either side. He reached the door
to Granger's, stopped to listen once again, then used the key
she'd given him.

The flat smelled neutral, no lingering scent of candles or
perfume that would have marked it on arrival as a woman's
home. The living room was tidy, with a kitchen visible across a
breakfast counter straight ahead, bedrooms and bathroom down
a hall to Bolan's left as he came in. Standing in her space, he
felt like an intruder, even though he had permission to be here.

Bolan was just about to tell her that the place was empty,
when the toilet flushed and heavy footsteps sounded, coming
toward him down the hall.

ROY MATTOX WASN'T sure if he should use the two-way radio
or not. On one hand, he wanted to know if the stranger they'd
seen on the street *was* their second target; on the other, if he
was the guy, squawking at Otto on the walkie-talkie might alert
their man before Otto could bag him.

Choices. Mattox hated them.

Just wait another minute, he decided, feeling clammy sweat
break out under his arms.

A minute couldn't hurt, right? Give the stranger time to get
upstairs and find the Ranger's pad, then…what? That was the
point where Mattox hit a snag and couldn't figure out what to
expect.

They'd seen the guy go in alone. The Ranger wasn't with
him, obviously, and she hadn't gone inside while they were

staked out in the parking lot, with Otto waiting in her digs. Assuming that the tall pedestrian *was* headed up to her apartment, did that prove he was their mark?

The Ranger was a woman. She could have a boyfriend, maybe more than one. No one had favored Mattox with a list of her acquaintances, much less their photographs. He knew the guy they'd seen wasn't another Ranger, since they all dressed cowboy-style, with big white Stetsons, pointy boots, the whole nine yards. Somebody else then. But he didn't want to kill the wrong guy and come out of this thing looking like an idiot.

He checked his watch. Still thirty seconds running on that minute he'd decided they should wait.

Now Mattox started wondering how Otto would react if somebody came knocking on the Ranger's door. His orders were to bag whoever *entered*. A simple visitor was something else, and popping out to deal with one could ruin everything. Some guy comes up to see the Ranger, maybe get a little action, and he finds a stranger in her flat. Next thing you know, he's phoning her—or worse, the cops—complaining there's a prowler on the premises.

Stay cool. He beamed the thought to Otto down the block, a waste of effort since he had no faith in ESP or much of anything, aside from firepower.

Another watch-check showed him seven seconds still remained on that minute. *To hell with it.* He picked up the radio and pressed the red send button with his thumb.

"Otto. You read me?"

Nothing.

"Otto! Do you copy?"

"He prob'ly turned the damn thing off," said Colin Page.

That made no sense to Mattox. Otto had checked in after he'd beat the Ranger's locks and gone inside. Trying the walkie one last time, he growled into its microphone, "Otto! Pick up, goddamn it!"

Still nothing.

"Let's roll," he told Ben Godwin, at the wheel. "No melodrama. Just pull up and park across the street."

Thinking, if he's asleep up there, I'll kick his ass from here to Sunday week.

And if he wasn't sleeping? Then what?

Mattox started adding two and two. Stranger goes in, and Otto loses contact. What was that, but trouble, pure and simple?

He could feel the setup starting to unravel, wondering if this was how the other teams had felt, in San Antonio and Arlington. Had they been confident at first, then seen the whole thing slipping through their fingers, realizing there was nothing they could do about it, no way they could save it? Had they realized their time was up, that they were dead men driving, flying or whatever?

Rotten thoughts. He tried to push them out of mind, but they were stubborn.

As it happened, there was no place on the west side of Clay Avenue to park the Jeep, but Mattox saw a slot across the street, two doors down from the Ranger's place, and pointed Godwin to it. Cursing, Godwin cranked them through an awkward three-point turn here in the middle of the block. Illegal, but there wasn't any cop around to make an issue of it as they doubled back and parked.

"Don't pull your guns until we get inside," Mattox reminded his two soldiers.

"What about my baby?" Page asked, holding up the submachine gun in its shopping bag.

Mattox hesitated for a heartbeat, then said, "Bring it."

"ONE DOWN."

As soon as Adlene Granger heard those words, she twisted the RAV4's ignition key and put the SUV in motion, rolling south on Webster Avenue, then turning left to join the one-way flow of traffic on South Fifth Avenue, driving one block before she made another left-hand turn onto Clay. First thing, she saw the Jeep Grand Cherokee was missing from its place outside the Stripes store on the corner, then she saw it parked near her apartment building.

Empty now.

There had been three men in the Jeep when Cooper had marked it on their first pass. Granger had not seen the vehicle, but pictured it from his description, relayed as she lay concealed in the Toyota. Cooper's report of one down told her that he'd found someone inside her flat when he had arrived, and he had handled it.

Whether the prowler was alive or dead, she wouldn't know until she went upstairs.

It made her skin crawl, thinking of a stranger prowling through her rooms, intent on killing her or worse. There was a sense of violation, but she had no time to focus on it now, with three more shooters headed up to join the party that had started in her absence.

There were no more parking spaces open on Clay Avenue, so Granger double-parked, blocking the Jeep Grand Cherokee from pulling out. Whatever happened in the next few minutes, even if the hit team slaughtered her and Cooper, they would be going home without their ride.

Granger thought briefly of her neighbors, all of whom should be at work. She took the big Benelli M4 Super 90 with her as she stepped out of the RAV4, taking care to lock it as she moved around the Jeep and hurried up the sidewalk, north-bound. Through the little gate and along the walkway she had trod a thousand times, up the concrete steps, and then she was inside.

No movement on the ground floor but a sound of voices muttering reached Granger's ears from somewhere on the second. She knew the stairs from long experience—which ones would always creak under her weight unless she placed her feet close to the wall. Climbing the staircase, Granger raised the shotgun to her shoulder, index finger of her right hand just outside the trigger guard in case she stumbled, since the safety was off, with a double-O round ready in the chamber.

Easy now.

When she confronted them, if they were in the hallway, it would be an easy shot. She'd give them a chance to drop their weapons, and when they refused—as she imagined they were bound to do—she'd squeeze off and keep on firing until all of them were down and dying.

There goes my security deposit, Granger thought, and swallowed back a laugh that came unwanted to her throat. More nerves than humor to it, in the present circumstances, as she climbed the next-to-last step and prepared to face her enemies.

The men who'd come to kidnap or to kill her.

"I'm here," she told the Cobra's compact microphone, almost a whisper, hoping Cooper could hear her. Either way, the time had come to make her move.

She stepped around the corner, shotgun leveled at three men standing outside the door to her apartment. Two were holding pistols, one a submachine gun, all fitted with silencers. The man nearest her door was leaning forward, as if listening, deciding what to do next, when she shouted out the only thing that she could think of.

"Texas Rangers! Drop your weapons! Now!"

BOLAN HAD DUCKED into the kitchen when he heard the toilet flush, down at the far end of the hall in Granger's flat. The guy who'd left his post to take a bathroom break came plodding back with no idea that anyone had entered while he dealt with nature's call, surprised as all get-out when Bolan pressed the Glock against his skull, behind his left ear.

"Do you want to live?" he'd asked.

"Uh-huh."

"Discard your weapons. Very carefully."

The guy had reached inside his blazer, pulling out a Springfield Armory XD autoloader with a suppressor attached to its muzzle. At Bolan's direction, he tossed it toward a nearby sofa, where it landed with a solid *thud*.

"What else?"

"That's it."

There'd been no point in asking him a second time, so Bolan clubbed him to the carpet, knocking him out cold. He used a pair of Granger's handcuffs to secure the shooter's wrists behind his back, then searched him, found a sap in his hip pocket and a short but wicked dagger in a boot sheath. Only then had he reported back to Granger, waiting on the street.

"One down."

A minute passed before a walkie-talkie sputtered on the fallen shooter's belt. "Otto. You read me?" Bolan let them wonder, and the caller came back: "Otto! Do you copy?" Finally, in something close to desperation, the voice ordered, "Otto! Pick up, goddamn it!"

Otto slept through it, and the little radio went dead. Bolan imagined the Grand Cherokee in motion, rolling toward him on Clay Avenue, its driver looking for a place to park. Granger would be approaching at the same time, in the RAV4, making an allowance for the hit team as they had agreed. Give them some lead time, so that they could enter the house and make their way upstairs. No showdown in the street if they could possibly avoid it. Keep the *High Noon* action to a minimum.

Bolan retrieved the silenced pistol from the sofa and examined it. The XD—for *X*-treme *D*uty—was also known as the HS2000, manufactured in Croatia and imported for domestic sales by Springfield Armory in Illinois. Otto What's-his-name had picked the XD Service model, chambered in .45 ACP, thirteen rounds in the magazine and one more in the chamber. Bolan put his Glock away and held the borrowed pistol loosely in his hand, waiting for company that he was sure must be approaching, even now.

It didn't take them long, all things considered. Bolan wasn't sure if they would have to drive around the block, seeking a parking spot, or if they'd leave their Jeep out in the street and rush the place. Bolan was listening, beside the door, when footsteps sounded on the stairs. He heard no conversation as the shooters closed in for the kill, uncertain what to make of the ongoing silence from their inside man.

With company outside the door, Bolan retreated, crouching down behind the sofa in the living room for cover, if they started firing through the older lath-and-plaster wall. The shooter he had knocked unconscious lay beyond the line of fire and relatively safe, at least until the door was breached. Bolan wished he could see how his opponents in the corridor were armed, but he would do his best to cope with whatever they threw at him.

In Bolan's ear, the lady Ranger's voice announced, "I'm here."

Inside, at least—but where, exactly?

As if she had heard his silent question, Granger shouted down the hallway outside her apartment, "Texas Rangers! Drop your weapons! Now!"

Somebody made a move, Bolan could almost picture it, and then he heard the big Benelli twelve-gauge. *Bam! Bam! Bam!* A man cried out in pain, as someone else burst through the door to Granger's flat, clutching a pistol in his hand. Wild-eyed, the new arrival spotted Bolan rising from behind the sofa, tried for target acquisition, was nowhere close to it when Bolan cut him down with two quick, nearly silent rounds.

Outside the open doorway, two more bodies sprawled, blood leaking into well-worn carpet. Neither one was moving as Bolan rose fully and called out through the door, "Adlene?"

"All clear," she answered back.

Up close, the buckshot had been merciless, and Bolan saw she'd winged the third man, too, before he had crashed the door. Now Granger stood above them, frowning at her handiwork.

"Sorry you won't get anything from these guys," she apologized.

"I've got a live one in the kitchen," Bolan told her. "Is there anything you want to pack before we go?"

"Could use some clothes," she said. "I won't be long."

Moments later, she was back, lugging the shotgun in her

right hand, with a smallish suitcase in her left. "I always keep a go-bag ready," she explained, "for callouts in the middle of the night."

"Good thinking," Bolan said. "Where are we parked?"

"Straight out and to the right."

"Go on ahead and get it running," he instructed. "I'll bring Otto down."

"Hope he won't miss his friends," said Granger.

"Not for long," the Executioner replied.

9

Highway Spur 412, McLennan County

The Shady Rest Motel had once been something special, patronized by visitors to Speegleville Park and Lake Waco, but time and the Texas Department of Transportation had passed it by. Business had slumped severely in the early 1990s, and petered out entirely by the time of Y2K. The place stood empty now, its fourteen individual cabins forever unoccupied, except by mice, insects and the occasional squatter.

Adlene Granger knew the Shady Rest from her patrols around McLennan County. Back in '04 there had been an ugly scene in Cabin No. One, involving teenage hitchhikers. "It was like something from a slasher movie," she told Bolan, while directing him to the motel. "Worst part, we never caught the guy—or guys—responsible. Kids say it's haunted now. Keeps most of them away."

Perfect.

He bypassed No. One and drove on to the end of the line, at Cabin No. Fourteen, parking the SUV behind it, where the vehicle could not be seen by any passing motorists. Their prisoner had floundered back to consciousness, moaning and cursing in the RAV4's rear compartment by the time Bolan had switched the engine off. They hauled him out and marched him to the cabin's door on wobbly legs.

"You want to pick it?" Granger asked him.

"Rather kick it," Bolan said, and snapped the cheap lock with a single application of his heel.

Inside the place was musty and smelled of rodents. Spiders had been busy decorating in the corners, and a lizard blinked in Bolan's flashlight beam before it skittered off the nightstand, racing toward the bathroom.

"When you've gotta go," Granger said.

"Lights?" he asked her, standing in the doorway.

"Not for years. Kids used to bring candles or lamps. I'm half surprised they didn't burn the whole place down."

"Okay. Dark works for me."

He walked their hostage to the bed and sat him down. "You have a last name, Otto?"

"What's it to you?"

"If you plan on coming out of this alive, you need to work on your rapport. Strike one was when you planned to kill my friend here. Strike two would be your attitude right now. Strike three...you're out."

"How will I know when I've got three?"

Bolan produced the silenced pistol he had taken from their prisoner. "You'll know," he said.

"Okay. My last name's Franks."

"You work for Lone Star?"

"Sometimes."

"How about today?"

A grudging nod.

"Some of your people took George Roth his from home today, in Dallas."

Now a shrug. "Don't know him," Franks replied.

Bolan tapped his shoulder lightly with the muzzle of the XD's silencer. "You really want to go for strike three?"

"Hey, man, I'm just a grunt, okay? You think I hang out with the Lone Star brass? I've never even *seen* the Big Man. Simon handles everything."

"That's Coetzee?" Granger asked him.

"Bingo. He's the one you should be talking to, if you want to know where they've got people stashed."

It sounded reasonable. "And we'd find him...where?" asked Bolan.

"Mostly he's with Ridgway. Has a pad in Dallas somewhere, but I've never seen it. He's on call 24/7. Anything comes up, he's on it."

"You know how to reach him," Bolan said, not asking.

"I've got his cell number. We all do. Not supposed to use it though, unless it's an emergency."

"You think this qualifies?" asked Bolan.

"All depends," said Franks.

"On what?"

"Your point of view. To me, okay. To Simon, not so much."

"Because you're just a grunt," said Granger.

"Facts of life," the prisoner replied. "A deal like this, you get jacked up, you're on your own."

Familiar rules. "Suppose you make the call and let me do the talking," Bolan said.

"You won't get anything from Simon."

"That's my problem."

"Not if he thinks I've been helping you," said Franks.

"I'll make it clear you haven't."

"What the hell. It's not like I can stop you anyway. Cell's in the inside pocket of my blazer."

Granger fished it out, a common model, handing it to Bolan. "Number?" Bolan asked their prisoner.

"Hit Speed Dial. Simon's first up on the list."

Bolan's thumb was on the button when Franks said, "You're killing me. You know that, right?"

"Right. But this is your lucky day." Bolan drove the butt of the XD into his prisoner's temple, rendering him unconscious. Franks would have to be put on ice until the end of the mission. The soldier would have to call in a marker.

Rivercrest, Fort Worth

THE NEWS WAS BAD. Again. On top of the two he had lost in the
helicopter crash, another three of his men were dead in Waco,
and a fourth was missing, presumed killed, as well; still no sign
of the Texas Ranger or the other target they'd been sent out to
eliminate. It was the kind of cluster-fuck that Simon Coetzee
hated, since it would reflect on him.

His men. His plan. His failure.

He could not recall another run of luck this bad since...well,
forever. He could blame the men he'd chosen, but that still came
back to him, since every member of his team was handpicked
for his training and experience. If they were failures, so was
Coetzee, by extension, for selecting them.

Blaming the targets wasn't working for him, either. Taking
out a Texas Ranger shouldn't have been difficult for any one of
Coetzee's soldiers, much less six and counting. Granted, he had
no idea who Adlene Granger's sidekick was, but who could she
have possibly recruited on short notice with the skills required
to fight his way through two of Coetzee's hit teams, plus the
squad fielded by Crockett down in San Antonio?

The bottom line: it didn't matter. Ridgway was expecting
him to solve the problem, and the only thing that Coetzee had
to show for it so far was five dead men for sure and one who'd
disappeared.

Which was a problem in itself. If Otto Franks was still alive,
if he was talking...

His cell phone came alive, playing the first three bars of *Die
Stem van Suid-Afrika*, his homeland's national anthem from
1957 to 1994, but then the communists took over and spoiled
everything. Coetzee checked the LED display and recognized
Franks's number.

"Franks, where are you?"

"Otto's indisposed right now," an unfamiliar voice replied.
It raised the hairs on Coetzee's nape.

"I see. Who am I speaking to?"

"A name won't help you find me."

"Then you won't mind sharing it."

Cold laughter came from the other end. "You sound like Cape Town," said the caller. "Or is it Johannesburg?"

"Neither these days," Coetzee replied. "I'm an American, like you."

The truth, in fact. Coetzee had passed the silly tests and had the paperwork to prove it.

"We're not the same," the stranger contradicted him. "I have no plans to start a half-baked country of my own."

Coetzee could feel a flush of angry color rising in his cheeks, but kept his voice under control. "I have no idea—"

"Cut the crap, all right? Why do you think I'm down here, playing tag with your toy soldiers?"

Swallowing the first response that came to mind, Coetzee said, "Why don't you explain it to me?"

"One on one, you mean? I wouldn't mind," the caller said, "but that still leaves us with the bigger problem."

"Which is?"

"What to do about your crazy boss, his rocket men and private army, the whole ball of wax."

"If I knew what you were referring to, but—"

"I can see why you'd eliminate Walraven," said the caller. "Once he made delivery on the fissile material, you might regard him as a liability. Roth, now, I'd say you still have use for him. But how much pressure do you think he'll take, before he cracks? Honestly, once he starts squealing, it'll be a toss-up whether old Lamar winds up in prison or a rubber room."

"You have a rich fantasy life," said Coetzee, nearly choking on the words.

"A fantasy you're killing people to protect and losing flunkies in the process. If anybody's keeping score, your side is ten men down so far."

"If you're convinced of what you're saying, you should speak to the authorities," Coetzee advised.

"I hate red tape, don't you? It's better to eliminate the middleman."

"Which means you have no case."

"And that would be a problem," said the caller, "if I was applying for a warrant. As it is, I'm doing fine, just whittling down your side."

In case the call was being taped, Coetzee inquired, "Are you confessing to the crime of murder?"

"Call it pest control."

"This has been amusing," Coetzee said, "but I'm a busy man. Unless you have some useful information for me…"

"Tell your boss he'll never have a country of his own to play with. If he's smarter than I give him credit for, he has a one-time-only opportunity to pull the plug. He can surrender and confess. Maybe he's got a shrink on tap who can convince the court he's just a senile lunatic."

"I really must be going now."

"You won't get far," the stranger said. And cut the link.

Coetzee's first impulse was to smash his cell phone, but he mastered that emotion and put the phone away.

It was a challenge then. And he intended to accept.

But first, the Big Man must be told.

Waco

"YOU THINK HE'LL CRACK?" Granger asked.

"No," Bolan replied. "But he'll report to Ridgway. Stir the old boy up a little anyway."

"If he's as crazy as I think he is, that may not be a good thing."

Bolan had considered that, but in his prior experience, pressing an enemy to act before he was fully prepared had frequently paid dividends. "We'll have to wait and see," he said.

"And in the meantime?"

"We have four potential targets. I'd prefer to leave Lone Star Petroleum alone for now," he said. "It seems to be legitimate—at least, as much as any other big oil company—and its facilities are widely scattered. Taking out refineries does nothing but pollute the landscape, and the corporation's office likely wouldn't give us much of anything."

"That's one."

"We could try the Lone Star Aerospace compound," he offered next. "Might stumble over Roth or knock their shuttle project off the rails. Against that, there'll be tight security with ready access to police, and not much chance of finding anything that would incriminate Ridgway."

"What's number three?"

"Go after Ridgway at his home, if he's still there. Try shaking something out of him or simply put him down."

"The down side being…what?"

"A man his age, if he's committed to this whole secession thing, he must have backup plans in place, to kick in if he doesn't cross the finish line. Crazy or not, he's old enough to know his time is running out. Who keeps the operation running if he dies or has a stroke, whatever? If he's thought through this at all, there'll be machinery in place to keep the oil and money flowing while his New Texas Republic gets up on its own two feet and learns to walk."

"You're talking like it's even possible," said Granger.

"To the men who've made the plans, it *is,*" Bolan replied. "Let's grant that they're delusional. That doesn't mean they haven't drawn up chains of command, contingencies."

"So, picking Ridgway off—"

"Would be like taking out the president. It's shocking, but it doesn't stop the government from operating or the military going off to war."

"Hands off the Big Man then?"

"I wouldn't go that far," Bolan replied. "Save him for later in the game."

"And what does that leave?" Granger asked him.

"Waylon Crockett and the NTR. We know Ridgway's been keeping them afloat financially, so he must have some use for them. Smart money says the leaders have an idea of what he's planning, maybe even how it's going down. And unlike Coetzee's men, the compound-dwellers won't be trained in methods of resisting an interrogation."

"We'd be going to their settlement outside San Angelo?"

"Is that a problem?" Bolan asked.

"Could be. You know it's not all goons with guns in there. Crockett has *families,* including wives and children."

"It's still doable," Bolan assured her. "Stealth, discretion, target acquisition."

"And if somebody starts shooting?"

"Take the shooters down. Limit the risk to bystanders."

"I notice you didn't say *innocent* bystanders."

"I'm not their judge," Bolan replied. "Let's say a wife adopts her husband's personal extreme agenda. Maybe it's the other way around. Espousing a belief is one thing. Acting on it bumps the ante. There's no race or gender to a finger on a trigger."

"What about the age?" she pressed him.

"I'll be going after Crockett and Luttrell, specifically," he answered. "If their bodyguards are children, then I'll make allowances. Beyond that, since I'm fresh out of explosives and your basic WMDs, it shouldn't be a problem."

"Oh? With children running all over the place?"

"Timing," he said. "We've got a good four-hour drive ahead of us, before we hit San Angelo. Say half an hour more to reach the NTR compound. I plan to stretch that out till nightfall, do my scouting in the dark, and let the kiddies go to bed before I make a move."

"Before *we* make a move," Granger corrected Bolan.

"Don't commit unless you're sure."

"Crockett may know who killed my brother," she replied. "I'm goddamned sure."

Preston Hollow, Dallas

"THIS IS A MAJOR disappointment, Simon. You do realize that, eh?"

"Yes, sir."

Lamar Ridgway was pacing as they talked, the cell phone pressed against his ear. Walking helped dissipate the nervous energy that filled him when he was frustrated, angry or depressed.

"What is your plan to remedy the situation, may I ask?"

"Sir, as we speak, four of my men are driving Dr. Roth to the facility. They'll have him under guard all day and bring him back again this evening."

"I would expect no less," said Ridgway. "But that isn't a solution."

"No, sir. I've increased security on Lone Star properties, and you'll have extra men around your home within the hour. Also our other friend."

A cryptic reference to Malcolm Barnhart, Simon taking extra care, even when they'd engaged the scrambler.

"Stop-gap measures," Ridgway said. "Still no solution."

"I'm continuing efforts to find the Ranger, sir. As for the man who called, presumably her backup, we have no I.D., and the cell phone he stole has been deactivated, which prevents using its GPS to track him."

"I want this problem settled, Simon. Lame excuses make me doubt the wisdom of employing you," Ridgway told his chief of security. "I've advanced the schedule. We announce tomorrow. Let the chips fall where they may."

Dead silence ensued for a moment, on the far end of the line, before Coetzee replied, "Yes, sir. I understand."

"Nothing must interfere with the arrangements. Do you hear me, Simon? *Nothing.*"

"Understood, sir."

"Act as if your life depends on our success," Ridgway advised. "Because it does."

He cut the link and left the cell phone on the bar, pouring himself a triple shot of Jameson's. The whiskey worked its magic on his jangling nerves but could not dampen the driving sense of urgency he felt.

Against his will and better judgment, Ridgway's plan had been advanced by action of his enemies—or, more precisely, through the failure of his soldiers in the field. He was not sorry for their deaths, per se. Ridgway believed that fools should suffer for their own mistakes, and he'd been spared the trouble of devising proper punishment. The public nature of the incidents, however, was a major inconvenience and had forced his hand before all aspects of his scheme were perfectly in place.

No matter.

They were close enough, he thought. The rockets and their shuttles—make that *warheads*—were as ready as they'd ever be. First thing tomorrow he would send his ultimatum out to Austin and to Washington, D.C. He didn't give a tinker's damn whether or not the White House recognized the New Texas Republic. That would come in time, he reckoned, when the lower forty-seven states were starved for gasoline. Right now it was enough for Ridgway's enemies to know that he could rain unholy hell upon them with the mere flip of a switch.

And if they doubted that…well, he might have to vaporize Manhattan, possibly Los Angeles, or maybe Washington itself.

Who'd really miss that rotten, lazy Congress, anyway?

His first shot might result in war, but Ridgway did not flinch from that idea. He knew damn well that Washington wasn't about to nuke Fort Worth or Dallas, whereas he had no compunction whatsoever about razing hives of miserable left-wing rot from sea to shining sea. Detroit, Chicago, San Francisco, Philadelphia, Miami—all fair game.

He'd fooled those vultures from the lamestream media with stories of his shuttle project and its single mighty booster rocket. That was all for show, a front, while George Roth and his team were building latter-day equivalents of the V-2. They had a dozen prepped for launching, each nose cone a knock-out punch for one of modern America's teeming urban cesspools. Given any reasonable choice at all, Ridgway preferred to hold those rockets in reserve.

But if his New Texas Republic was attacked, all bets were off. Welcome to Hell on Earth.

Of course, he had his own survival bunker ready, if it came to that.

Texas would definitely rise again.

San Angelo, Texas

THE TOWN WAS large enough for strangers passing through to go unnoticed on the street, the Goodfellow Air Force Base outside the city limits guaranteeing a steady supply of new faces. No one glanced twice at a somewhat dusty SUV with Texas plates, a normal-looking man and woman on their way to somewhere else.

Bolan and Granger stopped for dinner—supper, in these parts—at an old-fashioned drive-in on North Chadbourne Street. The place had carhops dressed like cowgirls, more or less, if anyone had ever busted broncos in faux leather miniskirts. Bolan took his chances on the house special, a half-pound cheeseburger with fries, while Granger had the pulled-pork barbecue. Milkshakes to wash it down and stand in for dessert.

They took their time over the food and let dusk settle in. Their plans, hashed out on the drive from Waco, could be modified according to the circumstances they encountered once they started scouting Waylon Crockett's compound. There was time to spare for their approach, reconnaissance and entry, taking one step to minimize collateral damage.

Some of that would depend on Crockett and his goons. In all the agonizing over Waco, back in '93, some people ignored the fact that twenty-odd members of the doomsday cult were shot by their fellow believers at point-blank range, with one three-year-old child stabbed to death. The ATF and FBI had taken major hits for their handling of that siege, and rightly so, but the story was never a one-sided tragedy.

Bolan planned to do better, but couldn't control the reaction of Crockett's armed guards. One nervous sentry with an automatic weapon could wreak bloody havoc in the compound before he was taken down. The same went for a cautious soldier, even one who marked his shots and made them count but couldn't stop a bullet passing through a target, flying on to cause more damage at a distance.

Caution was the key, but combat is notorious for spoiling best-laid plans.

When they were done with their meal, Bolan drove up North Chadbourne to the West Houston Harte Expressway, taking off westbound on Arden Road. He stuck with that until he reached South Burma—the road, not the country—then turned north and slowed on his approach to Crockett's compound, looking for a place to stash the RAV4 while they hiked the last mile in. It was full dark now, and Bolan killed his headlights as he nosed the SUV into a roadside stand of trees, concealed from passing motorists unless they stopped specifically to make a search.

They changed clothes in the shadows, one on either side of the Toyota, Bolan slipping into his skinsuit, while Granger settled for a pair of black jeans and a turtleneck to match, with a wool watch cap to confine her hair. In place of camouflage cosmetics, they used shoe polish from Granger's flat to darken hands and faces.

Heading out, Bolan wore both Glocks, plus the Springfield XD with its silencer and twelve rounds still remaining in the magazine. He took the Colt AR-15, while Granger carried the Benelli twelve-gauge loaded with eight rounds of double-O buckshot and spare shells in her pockets.

The last mile was a long, slow walk under a waning crescent moon, but as they neared the target, there were lights to guide them. Crockett's people didn't draw attention to the compound, but they kept a pair of pole-mounted security lights burning through the night, and several buildings still showed lit win-

dows as Bolan and Granger drew near. The pole lights let him
spot patrolling sentries on the camp's perimeter and map the
layout in his mind, comparing it to photos he had called up
on his laptop.

It was a town of sorts, all right, complete with water tower,
generators, public showers and latrines, a motor pool, a dining
hall and chapel, barracks for single men and smallish bungalows for families. The buildings Bolan could not readily iden-
tify were likely workshops, storage, possibly an arsenal. Some
of the property was under cultivation, raising vegetables, and
there were chicken coops at the south end.

Someone's idea of Eden in the desert, possibly.

About to come undone.

10

Waylon Crockett was starting to feel like a mushroom: people were keeping him in the dark and feeding him bullshit. And that had to stop.

Oh, sure, he understood the Big Man's attitude. His boys had screwed the pooch in San Antonio, all right, but so what? Ridgway, himself, was losing people right and left and he was still no closer to the Texas Ranger or her man of mystery. How was it Crockett's fault that Simon Coetzee and his so-called special forces couldn't pin down the couple?

The whole secession thing was Crockett's brainchild to begin with. Just ask the folks who knew him. He'd been preaching it for years before the idea started catching on with lazy pricks who thought signing online petitions was the end of it. A *gesture,* they would say. Call it *symbolic.* But the true-blue patriots were those who'd stockpiled guns and ammunition, dreaming of The Day, working around the clock to make it real.

Now it was coming, and the Big Man seemed to think that he could leave Crockett out of the loop.

One hell of a mistake.

Crockett took another swig of beer and said, "I'm callin' him."

Kent Luttrell replied, "Who, Coetzee?"

"Screw him. I mean Ridgway."

"I dunno, man."

"Don't know what?"

"Chances are you'll piss him off."

"He's pissin' *me* off! This whole thing's supposed to be *our* show, goddamn it! Mr. Big thinks he can just forget about us now. I'm here to tell you that he's wrong."

"I hear you," said Luttrell. "But things are tight right now. We've got the deadline moved ahead, this business with the Ranger and her boyfriend—"

"Not our fault!" said Crockett, interrupting him. "Has Coetzee managed any better with 'em?"

"No, but—"

"No! So why am *I* the goat? Our people dropped the ball, okay. Now his have dropped it *twice*. That oughta tell 'em somethin'."

"You know the way it works, though. Money talks."

"I'll tell you somethin', Kent, and you can take it to the friggin' bank. If anybody tries to cut us out of this deal—our *own* deal—we might just have to secede from *them*. See how they like it then."

"Sounds like a plan," Kent said, and took a long pull on his beer.

"I wanna think about this some," Crockett decided. "Figure out exactly what to say before I call 'im."

"Good idea," Luttrell said, nodding.

"Let the old man have an ultimatum, so he knows we're serious."

"I'm with you, Waylon. You know that."

"Remind him whose idea this was. Who oughta be in charge."

Crockett finished his beer, tried to remember if it was his third or fourth but couldn't work it out. Decided one more wouldn't hurt and reached into the cooler on the floor beside his chair.

"We shoulda gone after the Ranger and that other prick ourselves," he told Luttrell. "Just you and me."

"Woulda been sweet," Luttrell agreed.

"I'd love to get another crack at 'em," Crockett said. "Show Coetzee and Ridgway both what we can do."

"Too late for that, I guess," Luttrell replied.

"You never know." Crockett opened his beer and tossed its cap onto the table with his empty bottles. "They're still runnin' loose, the last I heard. Coetzee ain't bagged 'em yet."

"But with tomorrow—"

"It's a big day," Crockett granted. "But it's just another day. I guess the Ranger and her pal might skedaddle out of Texas, but suppose they don't? It's open season then, I say. And if the rest of 'em don't like it, they can go to hell."

"I'd better go 'n' take a turn around the compound," said Luttrell.

"You do that. And when you get back, we'll draw us up a plan."

THE COMPOUND'S FENCE was serious—chain-link with spikes and razor wire on top—but it was not electrified. Neither, on inspection, did it seem to have any alarms or sensors rigged to warn the compound's occupants of an incursion in progress. Just steel posts and wire, with roving patrols through the night.

Bolan had come prepared for that, with wire cutters and black twist ties. He'd scouted the perimeter with Granger, watching the patrols at work, getting their timing down. Two teams in Jeep Wranglers made the long circuit, driving in opposite directions, so that they passed one another every hour or so. Bolan had been expecting more security and was relieved to find that Crockett's team was negligent.

Bolan cut a flap in the chain-link, held it open for Granger to pass through, then used a couple twist ties to secure the wire behind him. It would pass a cursory drive-by inspection and would serve them as an exit when time came for them to leave.

And with an extra passenger, if they could pull it off.

The property sprawled over twenty-odd square miles, a rough quadrilateral with twenty-nine miles of fence for the Jeeps to patrol. Much of the land inside was cultivated, with corn on the side where Bolan and Granger had entered, the shoulder-high stalks offering cover as they hiked between the breached fence and the central compound. Sentries in the field would have been useful for security, but they met none as they advanced.

Strike two for Crockett and the NTR.

Bolan had wrestled with the notion that the lax security could be a trap designed to suck them in, but he'd seen nothing to support that during his reconnaissance. A fair bit of the compound proper had been visible as they had passed by the south end of the property, careful to stay clear of the only gate, and they had watched what seemed to be a small town rolling up its sidewalks for the night—minus the sidewalks. Stripped of all the guns and paranoia, it was basically a farming commune, early to bed and early to rise.

This wasn't Walden Pond, however. If you took away the crazies, there would be no settlement. The families fenced in here would have been living in the midst of civilized society, sending their kids to public school, thinking about their next paycheck or how to spend the weekend, rather than rebelling against Washington.

How many of them were convinced that they could pull it off?

It didn't matter in the long run. Bolan only needed one of them to take a ride with him and spill the compound's secrets. Waylon Crockett would be best and, failing that, his second in command. Beyond them it was guesswork, and the probe could prove to be a futile exercise.

So Crockett or Luttrell. Two targets. Otherwise, empty-handed withdrawal and a wasted trip.

Between surveillance photos and his recon on the spot, Bolan had singled out two bungalows as likely quarters for the men in charge. He thought the larger of them would be Crockett's, chosen as both status symbol and command post. The other, probably Luttrell's abode, would be their secondary target if the first one came up empty.

And if neither one was occupied tonight…then what?

Some scouting, if he thought that they could pull it off,

before they scuttled back to exit through the flap he'd cut in Crockett's fence. With any luck they wouldn't have to fire a shot, but if it came to fighting, Bolan was prepared.

And Granger?

She was steady when it counted, but he sensed that she was apprehensive about cutting loose where families might be at risk. That wasn't cowardice, just common decency. But if it hit the fan, she'd have to do whatever was required of her, to see the mission through.

A soft probe, sure, unless something went wrong and it turned hard.

They'd reached the far side of the cornfield, fifty yards out from the larger of the bungalows. Fifty yards of open ground, with nothing but the cool night to conceal them as they moved in for the pickup.

Starting now.

HEADING TOWARD the bungalow that Cooper had marked as Way-lon Crockett's likely living quarters, Adlene Granger was reminded of a bad recurring dream. She understood from reading up on such things that a variation of the same dream troubled many people: walking through some public place and suddenly discovering you were naked or, at best, dressed in some kind of skimpy underwear. Psychologists agreed that naked dreams related to a sense of shame or being unprepared for something, such as class assignments or a task at work.

The difference in this case was that Granger was awake, and while she wasn't nude, she *was* exposed, crossing the stretch of open ground between the tree line and their target. And this time, if she was discovered, she would not just be embarrassed. She'd be dead.

They caught a break with sentries, who apparently were only sent to cover the perimeter, instead of prowling through the settlement itself. Crockett had no guards on his bungalow—assuming it was his—and they reached it without incident, spending a moment in the prefab building's shadow, waiting to make sure no alarm was raised.

The bungalow was quiet, no lights showing through its windows. Granger followed Cooper as he crept to the building's southwest corner, peered around it toward the other nearby structures, then advanced to the front door. There was a porch light, but it hadn't been turned on. Cooper mounted two low wooden steps to reach the door and tried the knob.

It turned under his hand.

He turned to frown at Granger, slipped his rifle back onto its shoulder sling, and pulled the silenced pistol he had taken from Otto Franks. This was the moment where security alarms could ruin everything and put them in the middle of a swarming hornets' nest.

The door swung inward silently on well-oiled hinges. Cooper went in, and Granger followed, stepping quickly to one side. He closed the door behind her and produced a small flashlight, playing its narrow beam around the bungalow's front room. It was a combination living room and kitchenette. Ahead of them, two open doorways led to small bedrooms.

Both empty.

Where was Crockett?

"There's no bathroom," Granger whispered. "Maybe he went to the latrine?"

"Maybe," Cooper said.

"You want to wait for him?"

"Too risky," Cooper replied. "For all we know, he's shacked up or away on business. We could still be standing here at sunrise."

"So Luttrell?"

"If we can find him."

The bungalow had two front windows. Cooper and Granger checked them both for random passersby before they slipped outside and started toward the next one, which they'd pegged as likely housing Crockett's second in command. That one had lights burning in its front room, which should mean it was occupied, but Granger knew they couldn't verify that till they'd had a look inside.

Cooper took the lead again, while she brought up the rear, scanning the settlement by wan moonlight filtered through scudding clouds. She held the shotgun ready, just in case, but knew that if she had to use it, they were toast.

As they approached the second bungalow, Granger heard male voices and discovered that the nearest window on her side was open, with a screen in place to keep insects outside. Closing in was doubly risky now, since anyone inside, beyond the screen, could hear them if their feet scuffed on the dirt and gravel.

Step by cautious step, they reached the window, crouched beneath it, listening. The conversation wasn't quite an argument, but it was heating up.

"I don't like moving up the schedule," one voice said.

"He didn't have much choice," the other one replied. "This trouble—"

"Ain't our fault!"

"Did I say that?"

"*He's* sayin' it. Or thinkin' it, at least. You know he is."

"He gets in moods like everybody else."

"I don't!"

"Now, Waylon—"

"Tell me, when do *I* get in a goddamn mood?"

"How 'bout right now?"

"The hell you say? I got good reason to be pissed. It ain't some *mood* that just come over me from nowhere."

"No, but—"

"I was countin' on the month he gave us to get ready, Kent."

"We're ready as we need to be. After tomorrow there'll be plenty of time."

"Uh-huh. Unless there ain't."

Identities confirmed, Cooper was in motion, circling toward the bungalow's front door. Granger trailed him, hoping it wouldn't prove to be the last thing she ever did.

STEALTH OR SPEED? Controlling two men was a problem, when you wanted one or both of them alive. Bolan had hoped they would find Waylon Crockett on his own, maybe asleep, but now they'd have to deal with him *and* Kent Luttrell. Grab one and dust the other, hopefully without rousing the settlement at large.

Step one was getting through the bungalow's front door.

Still carrying the silencer-equipped XD, he tried the knob and felt it turn. There was no going back from that point, and he pushed through into light that made him squint after the outer darkness, taking in the scene. Beer bottles on a coffee table. Kent Luttrell reclining in a La-Z-Boy. And Crockett on his feet, retreating toward the unit's kitchen space.

There was a second when the New Texas Republic leaders gaped at Bolan and the lady Ranger coming in behind him, frozen, then it went to hell in hyperspeed. Crockett let out a yelp and bolted past the kitchenette, charged through the nearest bedroom door and disappeared. Bolan ran after him without a word, left Granger with Luttrell, and reached the bedroom just as Crockett dived headfirst through yet another window, taking out the screen and tumbling into darkness on the other side. Before Bolan could reach the window, Crockett was already off and running, shouting, "Red alert! Intruders! Red alert!"

Instead of going after him or trying for a long shot on the run, Bolan retreated to the living room. Luttrell was still kicked back in his recliner, hands raised high over his head, eyes focused on the bore of Granger's shotgun. His face had lost most of its color, and his mouth was hanging open, highlighting his need for major dental work.

"You want to live?" asked Bolan. He received a silent nod in answer. "Then get up and come with us," he ordered. "Try to run, you die."

"Okay."

Luttrell rose from his chair, an awkward moment aggravated by his trembling. Outside, somewhere in the compound, Crockett's cries for help were being answered. They were out of time and then some.

"I don't like our odds on foot," Granger observed.

"That's why we're taking wheels," Bolan replied. "Outside," he said to Luttrell.

He killed the lights as they were leaving, turning toward the compound's motor pool, where vehicles of several kinds were parked in tidy rows. "Where do you keep the keys?" he asked Luttrell.

"They're in the cars. Nobody's gonna steal 'em here," Luttrell replied.

"Better be true," Bolan advised their prisoner.

"If I'm lyin', I'm dyin'."

"You got that right," Granger confirmed.

They ran to the vehicles—no point in strolling casually now, and everything to lose if they were overtaken. Bolan picked a Wrangler, used by the sentries on their perimeter patrols, and slid behind the wheel. Granger shoved Kent Luttrell into the back and took the shotgun seat—quite literally in this case, half-turned with her twelve-gauge angled toward their prisoner.

The key was in its place, and Bolan twisted it, hearing the Wrangler's engine come alive. The fuel gauge registered at half a tank, but that was ample for his purposes. They had to breach the fence and get back to their waiting SUV, this time without a mile's slow hike through darkness from the highway.

If the compound-dwellers didn't kill them first.

Someone was shouting at them, coming closer, as Bolan put the Jeep in gear, released the clutch and powered out of there, working the stick shift smoothly. Bolan left the headlights off but couldn't stop others around the compound from blazing on, as Crockett's howling roused his soldiers and their families. Bolan and Granger's best hope now was to escape before women and children joined the pack.

"How are we playing this?" asked Granger, still faced backward, covering Luttrell.

"Straight through the corn," Bolan replied.

The ground they'd navigated while hiking in was dry enough to keep the Jeep from bogging down, and Bolan thought the

Wrangler should be able to plow through the stalks without stalling. He hoped so anyway.

They cleared the open ground and rows of corn loomed up in front of them. "Hang on," Bolan advised, and hit the green wall doing fifty miles per hour. In an eye blink, they were swallowed by the field.

Gunfire erupted as the Jeep rolled out of sight. Bolan glimpsed muzzle flashes in the rearview, there and gone as cornstalks blocked his view. The Wrangler made a poor target at night, unless he tapped the brakes, and—for the moment anyway—the last thing on his mind was slowing down.

The Jeep was not exactly a piece of farm machinery, but Bolan was impressed by its ability to clear the row of stalks he'd straddled when he drove into the field, tires churning up the irrigation troughs to either side. Corn rattled past the Wrangler's undercarriage with a sound like paper crumpling, and the Jeep was losing some of its momentum from resistance. Bolan stood on the accelerator, got its speed back up and held the steering wheel rock steady as he plowed ahead.

"They're coming after us," said Granger. "I see headlights."

Bolan caught a quick flash in his rearview mirror and ignored it. A pursuit had been inevitable from the moment Crockett had broken away from him. The question now was *how* they'd go about it. Would they follow Bolan's stolen Wrangler through the corn, or try to drive around and head him off? Was Crockett on a two-way radio already, summoning his guards from the perimeter to intercept them?

Probably.

"Be ready if they're waiting for us when we clear the field," he cautioned Granger.

"Got it," she replied. To Luttrell, she added, "One twitch, and you're a memory."

"No twitchin' here," he answered back. "Just watch that twelve-gauge, huh?"

"I'll watch it take your head off if you make a move," Granger replied.

"We're almost clear," Bolan said.

Then they were, the Wrangler leaping forward onto open ground once more, leaving the flattened corn behind. The rear-view mirror showed him headlights bobbing in the field, but Bolan focused on the pairs converging from his left and right, Jeeps drawn from their patrol around the fence by Crockett's radio alert. Two men per vehicle, which left one free for shooting on each side.

How would the sentries handle it, with Kent Luttrell on board? Was he expendable, or would they try to take Bolan and Granger back alive?

"Do what you can to slow them down," he said to Granger, aiming their Wrangler toward the chain-link fence, still something like a quarter-mile ahead. Another thirty seconds at their present speed.

"On it," said Granger, and he felt rather than saw her turning, to aim behind the driver's seat, toward the Jeep highballing from their left. He braced himself, leaned forward slightly, as Luttrell said, "Hey, now—"

Granger fired, the shotgun cannon-loud inside the small Jeep, taking out the left-rear window. Its ejected cartridge flew past Bolan, glancing off the steering wheel, and rolled across the Wrangler's dashboard.

"Missed 'em, damn it!" Granger said and fired again. More thunder, and the spent shell struck the inside of the windshield this time, bouncing back toward Bolan's lap.

Off to his left, the charging headlights veered away, then went into a crazy roll. Around the third flip, one light burst and left the other glaring like the lone eye of a Cyclops. Granger turned again, cranking her window down in preparation for a clean shot at the other Jeep.

That Wrangler's rifleman was firing at them now, short bursts from his side window, aiming awkwardly around the Jeep's wing mirror. Precision shooting wasn't feasible under the circumstances, but that didn't mean he couldn't catch a lucky break.

"Bastard!" said Granger, as she shifted the Benelli to her left hand, angling for a shot.

Bolan kept one eye on Luttrell in the backseat. No doors for him back there, and he was hanging on for dear life as they raced over rough ground, toward a collision with the compound's fence. He made some kind of muffled moaning sound, but Bolan couldn't pick out any words.

Granger squeezed off three shotgun blasts in rapid-fire, fighting the weapon's recoil, spent brass flying back to ping their ducking passenger. At least one of the shots hit home, and Bolan saw the second Wrangler swerve off course, not rolling like the first one, simply slowing as its driver slumped behind the wheel.

"Brace for it!" Bolan warned, and hit the chain-link doing sixty-five.

11

"What do you mean, you lost 'em?" Waylon Crockett raged.

"Jus' what I said," Sam Vandeveer replied, remembering to add a "sir" just in the nick of time. He was in charge of the community's security, and clearly knew his scrawny butt was on the line after the grim night's huge snafu.

Grinding his teeth, suppressing an impulse to strangle Vandeveer, Crockett said, "Now explain that to me, will you, Sam? How did you let 'em get away?"

"We didn't *let* 'em go. They took out both patrols, kilt two men doin' it and messed the others up real bad. They crashed the fence, then ditched the Wrangler by the highway, where they musta had another car waitin'. We chased 'em through the corn, you know, but they was gone before we made it to the road."

"And took Kent with 'em."

"Well...I guess."

"You *guess?* Where else you think he went, up to the freakin' mother ship?"

"I only meant—"

"Don't say another goddamn word! Your people missed 'em out on the perimeter and let 'em walk right through the compound to my goddamn door!"

"Lucky you wasn't there," Vandeveer said.

"Lucky? Did you say *lucky?* It was only by the grace of God they didn't snatch me up, along with Kent!"

"They didn't, though."

"You think that makes it better? That it gets you off the hook?"

"Um..."

"Stop gruntin' at me, damn it! Do you know how they got in here in the first place?"

"Yessir. They cut the fence," said Vandeveer, "then wired it back together."

"And your people didn't notice that?"

"They did a good job. Wasn't obvious, unless you knew what you was lookin' for."

"Which no one did, until their dirty work was done."

"Them two are slick. I'll give 'em that."

Sometimes it took the patience of a saint to deal with idiots. "So you admire 'em now," said Crockett.

"Well, I wouldn't say—"

"You understand they have Luttrell? Has that sunk in?"

"Yessir, I understand."

"They could be squeezin' him for information right this very minute. This could ruin everything."

"I'd say he's purty tough," Vandeveer said.

"You would, huh? Maybe I should kick you in the balls and see how tough *you* are. How'd that be?"

"Don't suppose I'd like it," Vandeveer allowed.

"Tell you what *I* don't like," said Crockett. "Since I called this in to Simon, now I gotta go and see him personally, to explain how we screwed up. You're goin' with me, Sammy."

"I ain't sure if—"

"Don't mistake it for an invitation," Crockett told him. "It's a goddamn order!"

"Yessir. Right. Okay."

"We're leavin' in five minutes. Anything you gotta do, see to it in a hurry."

"Yessir."

Vandeveer was none too happy when he left, which suited Crockett to a tee. He didn't plan to take the rap for this alone, if he could serve somebody else up as a sacrifice to Simon Coet-

zee's wrath. The most important thing, to Crockett, was survival—and the place he'd been promised in the new order that
would arise when Ridgway played his hole card. Once they'd
passed that crisis, Crockett would be golden. He could write
his own damn ticket in the New Texas Republic.

And if that meant he had to pull the plug on Vandeveer, so
be it. He'd already lost Luttrell, no realistic hope of ever seeing him alive again, so why not cut some deadwood? Vandeveer had let him down, made him look foolish, nearly cost
Crockett his life.

Some things, as Sammy was about to learn, were unfor-
givable.

Coleman County, Texas

ROLLING EAST ON I-67, Bolan spotted a deserted-looking barn
and pulled off the highway and drove along an access road
that was more weeds and dirt than blacktop until he found a
place to park behind the sagging structure, out of sight of traffic on the interstate. He killed the RAV4's lights and engine,
spent a moment listening to night sounds from the desert, then
stepped out.

Granger hauled Kent Luttrell out of the backseat, and Bolan
helped her direct their captive toward the barn, sweeping the
ground before them with a flashlight beam. Field mice were
plentiful, which made him think of snakes, but they encountered none before they reached the barn and entered through
a gaping doorway. What had happened to the door was anybody's guess.

It had been close, escaping from the compound, but he'd
managed to outrun their various pursuers after Granger had
discouraged the perimeter patrols. Once they were back in the
Toyota, it came down to speed and running without lights the
first couple miles, then slowing down and driving normally
across the northwest part of Concho County into Coleman.
Bolan didn't know if Crockett would resort to notifying law

enforcement, but he doubted it, and sixty-odd miles seemed far enough to run, as long as they could find a decent hiding place.

Which they had.

The barn was filled with dust and spiderwebs, more rodents rustling in abandoned stalls and overhead, in what had been the hayloft. Shafts of dim moonlight were visible through large holes in the roof, and Bolan guessed that bats might roost up there during the daylight hours. Maybe doves and other birds, as well. Devoid of neighbors, isolated in the night, it was as good a place as any to interrogate Kent Luttrell.

As if in tune with Bolan's thoughts, their prisoner chimed in. "So this is it? You gonna tell me what it is you want?"

"Give us your best guess," Bolan answered.

"Beats the hell out of me."

"That's funny," Granger said, "since you've had pecker-woods trying to kill us over half the state."

"Says who?"

"The only thing you'll get from playing dumb," Bolan advised him, "is a bullet."

"Way I see it, if you meant to snuff me, I'd be dead already. Drivin' me out here, wherever this is, tells me you want somethin' else."

"Not as dumb as he looks," Granger said.

"Screw you, bi—"

She clubbed him down with the Benelli's stock, dropping the captive to his knees. Luttrell spat blood and something Bolan thought might be a molar.

"Shit!"

"The tongue still works," said Granger.

"You're mighty tough," Luttrell said, "when it's two on one and you got all the guns."

"The way it was with Jerod," Granger said.

"Who's that?"

"My brother. You remember sending goons to kill him?"

"I ain't killed nobody," said Luttrell.

"I guess you never heard of double negatives."

"Say what?"

"He's all yours," Granger said to Bolan. "I can't stand the sight of him."

"Just tell me what you want," Luttrell whined, spitting out more blood. "Then get me to a doctor, will ya?"

"George Roth, for starters," Bolan said.

"Don't know the man."

Luttrell was struggling to his feet when Bolan squeezed the XD's trigger and a nearly silent slug drilled through the captive's left kneecap. Luttrell screamed as his leg gave way and dumped him back into the dirt. Bolan stood watching him until the sobbing trailed away to whimpers.

"George Roth," he repeated.

"Christ! Okay! Aw, shit," he growled, clutching his shattered kneecap. "I'll talk. What…do you…wanna know?"

Desdemona, Texas

SIMON COETZEE HAD agreed to meet Crockett halfway, in sparsely populated Eastland County. The county's population had dropped, from close to sixty thousand in the 1920s, down to roughly eighteen thousand at the last census, and almost no one lived in Desdemona, a certified ghost town on State Highway 16, twenty miles west of Stephenville.

It was the perfect place for tying up loose ends.

Coetzee had come alone but well prepared. Beside him on the passenger's seat of his BMW X5, a Heckler & Koch MP5K-PDW machine pistol lay covered with a copy of the *Dallas Morning News.* This version of the weapon included a side-folding stock, selective fire permitting three-round bursts and a muzzle threaded to accommodate suppressors. Beneath his left arm, he'd hung a SIG Sauer P250 semiauto pistol with a recessed hammer and a double-action-only trigger, chambered for the same 9×19 mm Parabellum rounds as his machine pistol. Between the two guns, he had fifty rounds ready to go without reloading.

More than enough for one man or two.

Waiting, he lit the last of seven cigarettes he allowed himself per day, when time permitted. Self-denial had nothing to do with character development in Coetzee's case, much less spirituality. He simply made a point of keeping his desires under control and doing nothing to excess, a constant test of his personal resolve. While others often disappointed him, it had been years since Coetzee had been disappointed in himself.

The ghost town did not trouble him. He knew its dreary story: once a thriving oil camp, back around the First World War, its field played out during the early 1920s, and the mastermind behind it went to prison for defrauding his investors. The town wasn't *exactly* dead today, of course. But there'd be no one to disturb him when he met with Waylon Crockett on the town's outskirts.

Not even ghosts.

Coetzee spotted a pair of headlights coming from the west and flicked his cigarette away, sliding a hand beneath the *Morning News* to find the pistol grip of his MP5K. The question now was whether he should chat with Crockett for a little while or just get down to business. Coetzee thought about it and decided he would let the circumstances be his guide.

An SUV pulled up beside him, Crockett looking sour in the shotgun seat, and a face Coetzee had never seen behind the steering wheel. The driver's window powered down, and Coetzee spoke across him, saying, "So you brought a friend?"

"Can't be too careful these days," Crockett answered.

"Sad but true," Coetzee agreed.

He climbed out of the BMW X5, no dome light's glare behind him as he straightened up and sprayed the SUV's two passengers with half a magazine of Parabellum rounds. It was a messy way to die, but none of it blew back on Coetzee, and he'd spared himself the tedium of small talk going nowhere.

Cleaning house.

He looked in both directions, up and down the long, dark highway. When he had satisfied himself that he was still alone—at least among the living—he put the MP5K back under the newspaper and palmed a small incendiary stick. He then opened the gas cap cover on the SUV, removed the cap itself and left it dangling while he primed the stick, then stuffed it down the fuel tank's filler neck.

The BMW roared to life a moment later, powered through a U-turn and had cleared a long block eastbound when the gas tank blew. Smiling at his own reflection in the rearview, Coetzee turned on the radio. Caught Billy Joel in the middle of "We Didn't Start the Fire."

"So true," he told the night.

But fire was coming, and he wondered whether anyone in Texas—or the country, for that matter—would emerge unscathed.

Coleman County

ONCE HE FOUND the strength to speak again, Luttrell spilled everything. He didn't know where they could find George Roth, but that small lapse paled by comparison to what he could tell them about Ridgway's operation and the oil man's plan for setting up a New Texas Republic. It was a bizarre scheme, bound to fail in Bolan's estimation, but with a grim potential for disaster.

Lying in the dirt, clutching his shattered knee, Luttrell explained in fits and starts. "That stuff about the moon is all bullshit. Lamar picked up a shuttle on the cheap and had his people build a bogus booster ride. The real deal is his other rockets."

"*Other* rockets?" Bolan prodded.

"Smaller 'n what they use to send a shuttle up, but big enough to fly across the country. Maybe hit New York or Washington, maybe L.A. or Frisco. Got his warheads ready, courtesy of Uncle Sam, who don't keep track so well."

"And Ridgway keeps these where?" asked Granger.

"Lone Star Aerospace. I never got the tour, myself," Luttrell explained, "but Waylon's seen 'em. Says they got a setup over there makes Cape Canaveral look like a broke-down movie set."

"That's his muscle for the ultimatum," Bolan said, thinking out loud.

"You got that right," Luttrell agreed. "After he fires that warnin' shot, nobody's gonna mess with Texas anymore."

"What warning shot?" asked Bolan.

"Little somethin' just to wake 'em up in Washington."

"When is this warning shot supposed to happen?" Bolan asked the wounded man.

"*Supposed* to be next month," Luttrell replied. "But you-all bumped it up, see? Now it flies tomorrow, while the Big Man's talkin' on TV tellin' the world to kiss his ass."

"So what's the target?" Bolan asked.

"Dunno." Luttrell was sounding groggy now. "It's like a game to him. Play spin the bottle. Throw darts at the map. The lucky winner is…whoever."

"When's this happening tomorrow?" Granger asked.

"When else? High noon."

Granger was looking at her watch. "Nine hours and change," she said.

No time to waste then. Lone Star Aerospace was based outside of Houston, 280 miles southeast of Coleman County. Say four hours on the road, if they started with a full tank of gas and held a steady seventy miles per hour all the way.

Granger had obviously done the calculations for herself. She said, "We need to go. Right now."

"Hey, what about that hospital?" Luttrell asked, blinking up at them.

"I'll see what I can do," Bolan said.

"It'll be daylight by the time we get to Houston," Granger said, as they were exiting the barn.

"Can't help it," Bolan told her. "We'll plan something on the way."

To pull the plug on Armageddon, right. If they could manage it.

Climbing into the Toyota, Granger said, "I keep thinking there should be someone we can call."

"Maybe there is," Bolan replied.

Preston Hollow, Dallas

"I MUST SAY, Crockett disappoints me."

"Past tense," Simon Coetzee corrected.

"Of course," Ridgway agreed. "But still. I thought he had more grit. It all came down to nothing in the end."

"What do you want to do about his people?" Coetzee asked.

"Nothing for now," Ridgway replied. "After tomorrow they can join us or remain inside their fence until they starve, for all I care."

"Big day," Coetzee observed.

"The biggest." Ridgway sipped his Jameson Rarest Vintage Reserve.

In fact Ridgway had been looking forward to this day all his life, even before he had recognized the final goal. For years he had thought that making money was enough, an end unto itself, but he'd been wrong. When he'd become involved in politics, it had gradually dawned on him that nothing could be changed—not for the better, anyhow—unless he personally took control and forced the change himself. Deciding *how* that should be done consumed more years, but Ridgway had the answer now. Tomorrow he would share it with the world at large.

And screw 'em if they didn't like it.

"Has a target been selected yet?" asked Coetzee.

"I'm still workin' on it," Ridgway said. "So many cesspools of corruption, so little time."

In truth, of course, he'd prospered from corruption—buying politicians, judges, juries, lawmen—and he wouldn't change that if he could. It was the *other* kind of decadence that raised his hackles: all the things that leftists talked about as signs of "progress." Pick a poison from the commie shopping list or lump it altogether as "diversity." Whatever. With the rank malarkey of political correctness stripped away, it all boiled down to weakening America, the one-time greatest nation in the world.

For decades Ridgway had believed that he could save America by funding this or that group on the Right. The second decade of the new millennium had changed his thinking on that subject, made him realize America was lost for good. Only a new start, on a smaller scale, could rescue what remained of values passed down from the founding fathers. He, Lamar Ridgway, could make that change.

Why else had God allowed him to become a billionaire?

"When are you flying down?" asked Coetzee.

"*We* are flying down in just over an hour. If you need to pack, it's time."

"You don't want me to stay and track the hunt?"

"Forget it. In a few more hours, if those pesky little shits are still around, they'll wish they'd run while they could still get out."

"Okay. I'll call ahead and have security in place for our arrival."

"Everybody works today," said Ridgway. "No excuses."

"Yes, sir."

Ridgway finished off his whiskey, thought about pouring another shot, then decided that he'd better not. He wanted to amend his statement to the world, kept thinking of new items he should add. It needed to be exactly right.

As it turned out, hijacking radio and television broadcast satellites was no big deal, once he'd acquired the best minds in the business and equipped them with the latest gear. A lot of it was gibberish to Ridgway—direct broadcast versus fixed service satellites—but hell, he didn't have to understand it, as long as the damn system worked on command. They'd done a test run for radio two months earlier and then TV last month. A simple blip in each case, service very briefly fading in and out, but it had been enough to demonstrate the power at his fingertips. Sources in Washington informed him that the FCC had been "concerned" but couldn't trace the source of interference either time.

Tomorrow, naturally, there would be some stations that he couldn't interrupt, and that was fine. Their news departments would report his ultimatum in their own good time. And once he'd fired his warning shot, the whole world would be watching.

That was power.

And it rested squarely in his hands.

Arlington, Virginia

BROGNOLA FREQUENTLY WORKED LATE, but not this late. The phone that woke him from a pleasant dream of deep-sea fishing was inside a drawer on his nightstand, the drawer in question just below a clock that showed him the ungodly hour. Already wide awake, he reached the phone on its third trilling note and raised it to his ear.

"Brognola."

"Striker," the familiar voice replied.

"This can't be good."

"It's worse than that," said Bolan. "Are we scrambled?"

Hal's thumb found a button in the darkness. "Got it."

"Ridgway's building rockets. Has them built already, I should say. Not ones for shuttle flights but multiple ballistic missiles, armed with warheads."

Hal experienced a chill, as if someone had poured ice water down his back. "What range?" he asked.

"Unknown. My best guess would be intermediate to long."

Translation: they could reach most cities in North America.

"Present location?"

"I'm working on the premise that it's Lone Star Aerospace in Houston, but that hasn't been confirmed," Bolan said.

Hal's mind was racing. "I'm not sure how much I can do. There are some people I can call, but whether they can move or not is problematic."

Everybody knew that 9/11 had revised the way America responded to terrorist threats. It had spawned the U.S. Department of Homeland Security and the Patriot Act, legalized all kinds of domestic surveillance, created secret prisons and "enhanced interrogation" centers—the list went on and on. But there were still some things that wily politicians would not do, and one of those was send a SWAT team after an eccentric billionaire with friends in Congress, on the basis of a vague call in the middle of the night, from an informant whom Brognola couldn't even name.

"There's NEST," Bolan suggested.

"Right. I'll call them first and put them on alert."

NEST was the Nuclear Emergency Support Team, a branch of the National Nuclear Security Administration tasked with investigating illegal use of nuclear materials on U.S. soil.

"Ridgway has a deadline," Bolan told him. "Noon today."

Hal felt his stomach tighten. "That's a launch time?"

"If my information is correct," Bolan replied. "Coordinated with some kind of public ultimatum."

"Do you have a target?"

"Sorry," Bolan said. "My source wasn't that high on the food chain."

Hal logged the warrior's use of past tense. He gathered Bolan's source would not be granting any further interviews.

"Okay," Brognola said. "I'll work with what we have. There's always Delta in a pinch."

Delta Force—the U.S. Army's First Special Forces Operational Detachment-Delta—was the go-to group for emergency counter-terrorist action, sometimes operating in conjunction with its counterparts, the U.S. Navy's Naval Special Warfare Development Group and the Twenty-Fourth Special Tactics Squadron of the U.S. Air Force. Among those units, Hal was confident that he could find someone to tackle a nest of rogue missiles. The question wasn't *if,* but rather *when.*

Right now Mack Bolan was his best—his only—hope.

"You're on it then," Hal said, not asking.

"On my way," Bolan confirmed.

"I'll see what I can do at this end," Hal assured him.
"Right," the grim voice answered.
And the line went dead.

12

Interstate 45, Southbound

Interstate 45 is a peculiarity in that it, despite its name, crosses
no state lines. It runs from Dallas to Houston, then continues
briefly to the Gulf of Mexico over the Galveston Causeway.

Today it served the Executioner.

Texas lawmakers had done him an unintentional favor in
2012, boosting the speed limit on I-45 to seventy-five miles
per hour. Bolan pushed it up to eighty, trusting lax highway
patrolmen and Adlene Granger's badge to keep him out of
trouble on the run to Houston, shaving half an hour off his estimated travel time.

It would have been a quicker trip if they were flying, but
he'd estimated that the time it took to find a charter service,
prep a plane and reach the nearest airport would have eaten up
the difference. So they were driving, starting with a full tank
in the RAV4, rolling through what some reporters called the
Texas Killing Fields.

No one would know it watching the landscape pass, but the
highway was notorious for a series of unsolved murders. Since
construction was finished in 1971, the bodies of at least thirty
girls and women had been found about a mile off the interstate.
It was easy to believe that more undiscovered graves still remained throughout the countryside.

"I worked this case, you know," said Granger. "Cases, I
should say."

"And still no break?"

"One guy went down for five, around the time I joined the Rangers. Media called him the Tourniquet Killer, after the way he strangled his victims. He's on death row currently, but the rest are still cold cases. It feels weird now, thinking that none of that may mean a hill of beans, if Ridgway flips a switch."

"He won't," Bolan asserted. "We'll stop him."

"Any thoughts on how?" she asked.

"We need to verify our information from Luttrell before we move."

"Sounds like another snatch job," Granger said.

"Maybe with a twist. Lone Star should be well-staffed with security."

"Which helps us…how, again?"

"I'll have to check their setup, but smart money says they'll have I.D. and a communications system."

"So?"

"If we can penetrate it," Bolan said, "we've got our way inside."

"You have a plan for doing that?"

"I'm working on it. First thing we need to do, once we're in Houston, is rent a van."

"Because?"

"It's more convenient than an SUV for what I have in mind," said Bolan. "Larger doors for better access, not to mention privacy."

"Okay. You're sounding like a psycho-killer now."

I've been called worse, he thought, but kept it to himself. She wouldn't understand the reference, and there was no point opening that door to Bolan's buried past.

"It's strategy," he said. "That's all."

"Don't get me wrong," Granger replied. "I'm in. I'd like to know the plan before the shooting starts, is all I'm saying."

Bolan sketched it for her, laying out what he'd devised so far, reminding her that its success depended on security deployment when they got to Lone Star Aerospace. His preparations might turn out to be a waste of time, in which case they would have to try a more direct approach.

"Oh, *more* direct," she answered, smiling ruefully. "Like kamikaze-style?"

"Let's leave that for a last resort," he said.

"I normally don't go for hara-kiri on a first date," Granger said.

"Point taken," he replied. "I wouldn't want to spoil your record."

"But it still might come to that."

"Don't focus on worst-case scenarios right now."

"I get it. Still, needs of the many. I'm just saying."

And the Executioner had been there, sure. So far he'd always walked away.

So far.

George Bush Intercontinental Airport, Houston, Texas

THE FLIGHT FROM Dallas to Houston took thirty-five minutes in Ridgway's Learjet 60, powered by twin Pratt & Whitney Canada PW300 engines. He flew in luxury, as always, with a twentysomething flight attendant seeing to his every need almost before the thought occurred to him. Besides Ridgway, the jet's passengers included Malcolm Barnhart, Simon Coetzee and six of Coetzee's handpicked security men. Another half-dozen soldiers were waiting for Ridgway on the airport's tarmac, with three black Humvees that would carry his party to the Lone Star Aerospace plant west of town.

The flight was uneventful, just the way he liked it. No one wanted any kind of incident when they were cruising eight miles high, much less when they were focused on a looming date with destiny. Ridgway thought Barnhart looked uneasy, but he'd never had a spine of steel.

In fact his malleability was a critical attribute for a puppet.

He had agreed without demur to Ridgway's guidance in their planning for the New Texas Republic, interested chiefly in attaining a preeminent position and the wealth that went along with it. Barnhart understood what was expected of him and would soon hold honors as one of the world's best-paid yes-men.

Always assuming that they managed to survive the next few days.

There was a chance, Ridgway supposed, that the usurper in the White House would display more courage than Ridgway had counted on. The New Texas Republic would be starting small, in terms of military strength, but Ridgway thought his warning shot, together with the clear and present danger of a backup salvo fired from coast to coast, would keep the hounds at bay. If he was wrong…

Well, it would be an interesting day or two, and even when the Green Berets or Navy SEALs, or whoever, took him down, he would have changed the world. When histories of the event were written, he would be remembered as the man who cleansed America with fire and gave those of its people who remained a chance to start from scratch, rebuilding on the model of the *good old days.*

Why not?

Who in his right mind would repeat the grievous errors of the past half century, when the results of ceding freedom to a mongrel welfare state were clearly recognized? How many nations got a do-over like that? Only a handful in recorded history, and none at all since World War II.

A stranger to false modesty, Ridgway believed himself to be the savior of America, perhaps the world. Whether he won or lost the greatest gamble of his life, he'd never be forgotten.

Hell, he'd be *revered.*

George Roth was waiting for them at the plant, flown down the night before by Coetzee's team, to get the final preparations underway. He'd done a great job on the rockets, building on his grandpa's V-2 model to create a deadly no-frills arsenal. They had a dozen primed to fly, with twice as many in production, just in case.

The rockets' simple mechanism used the classic ethanol/water mixture for fuel, and liquid oxygen as an oxidizer. The combustion burner fired at a temperature of 4,500 to 4,900 degrees Fahrenheit. Guidance was achieved by four external rudders on the tail fins, and four internal graphite vanes at the motor's exit, while two free gyroscopes provided lateral stabilization. At engine shutdown, sixty-five seconds after launching, a program motor controlled the pitch to a specified angle, dropping into a ballistic free-fall trajectory from fifty miles up.

Then *ka-boom!*

Ridgway was looking forward to that mushroom cloud with mixed emotions.

Mostly, if he were honest, he was proud.

Robert F. Kennedy Department of Justice Building, Washington, D.C.

AFTER HIS WAKEUP call from Bolan, Brognola dressed in haste and hurried to his office, dodging predawn traffic, cell phone grafted to his ear. His first call went to Stony Man Farm and put the whole team on alert. They would use every resource available to confirm the site of Ridgway's would-be launch-pad without crossing the line and possibly triggering a premature liftoff. That included satellite surveillance of the Lone Star plants in Texas and—a long-shot gamble—oil rigs in the Gulf of Mexico that might conceivably disguise a missile silo.

Doubtful, but in this nightmare scenario, nothing could be ruled out.

After arriving at his office, Hal called the NNSA's headquarters on Independence Avenue. That was the only way to mobilize NEST, a far-flung network of some six hundred specialists with regular day jobs at various universities, research laboratories and government agencies. It would take time to roust them from bed and brief, gather and prepare them for what might turn out to be—God willing—just another false alarm.

The NNSA's nearest site to Houston was the Pantex Plant, America's only nuclear weapons assembly and disassembly facility, located northeast of Amarillo in the Texas Panhandle. That placed it almost six hundred miles north of Houston, while the nearest military installation was Truax Field, the Naval Air Station at Corpus Christi. That was 184 miles from Lone Star Aerospace as the F-35 Lightning II multirole fighter flies, nine minutes from takeoff to payload delivery in the worst-case scenario.

Worst case for whom?

If Ridgway landed the first punch, its impact would depend on the warhead his rocket carried. The atomic bomb dropped on Hiroshima in 1945 had killed an estimated eighty thousand people when it detonated, vaporizing buildings close to a mile from the blast's hypocenter. Another two hundred thousand people had died over the next several years, from burns, injuries or radiation sickness. Citizens were still developing cancer directly linked to radiation exposure into the twenty-first century. Depending on the target Ridgway chose, the death toll from a nuclear strike could range from thousands into millions, with property damage off the Richter scale. And there was bound to be retaliation, though Hal doubted that the president would order nuclear reprisals against Texas. The Lone Star plants were bound to fall, with hundreds—maybe thousands—buried in the wreckage of a madman's empire. As for the political and social shock waves, would they ever fade away, in a region where some people still believed they should have won the Civil War in 1865?

It was too much for Hal to think about right now. The NNSA's duty operator patched him through to the agency's director, waking him as Bolan had woken Brognola. It was the director's job to scramble NEST and have its experts standing by, ready to move whether the gambit Bolan planned was a success or tragic failure.

Either way Brognola knew there would be blood.

The burning questions now were how much and whose?

Lone Star Aerospace Technology, Houston

GEORGE ROTH STOOD beside the rocket he had come to think of as his child. It towered forty feet above him, fourteen tons of sleek and shining death, prepared to soar aloft at 3,500 miles per hour, then plummet toward impact with its chosen target. Roth still did not know where it would land, and truth be told, he didn't care.

Destruction was its own reward.

The rocket would not launch from where it stood, its last preflight inspection underway. Rather, Roth had adapted the technique devised by his grandfather and others during the glorious days of the Reich, building a modern version of the venerable *Meillerwagen.* The souped-up trailer would transport the missile and erect it on a firing stand, but it would also serve double-duty as the supply tower to fuel up and prepare the rocket for liftoff. The carriage, with its towing arm, was forty-nine feet long and tipped the scales at nearly thirteen tons.

The old V-rockets had been named *Vergeltungswaffen* in his native German—reprisal weapons. The label still applied today. Revenge had been a long time coming for the decadent American society that had destroyed the Reich, uprooting Herman Rothmann and his family from their homeland, but it had never been forgotten. Handed down from father to son and grandson, the goal of striking back would finally be realized.

Today.

Roth personally had no interest in Lamar Ridgway's plans for a New Texas Republic. To Roth, no part of the United States was any better than the rest, though some of the initiatives adopted in Texas during recent years reminded him of stories he had heard about the 1920s and early 1930s. There were private armies on the march, a spirit of defiance in the air. Roth would personally be delighted if his rocket fell on Washington, but any target would be satisfactory.

As long as he could watch America convulse in pain.

"He's here!" someone called out across the vast hangar. "Everyone in place!"

Roth turned to watch Ridgway approaching, flanked by Malcolm Barnhart and their troupe of bodyguards. The little bantam rooster of a man had helped Roth realize his lifelong dream, but he could never think of Ridgway as a friend. At heart the Big Man was too crass, too addicted to his wealth, too all-around *American* to rank among Roth's pantheon of heroes.

Ridgway was approaching now, a broad smile on his face. He pumped Roth's hand. "Are we ready?"

"Yes, sir. Absolutely," Roth assured him. "Relocation to the firing site and fueling should require no more than forty minutes."

"Excellent! We'll have it airborne in the middle of my broadcast then."

"As planned, sir."

"And what about the MDA?"

The Missile Defense Agency had been established in the early eighties, to create a layered defense against ballistic missiles. The agency was designed primarily to spot missiles launched at the United States from foreign countries as distant as Russia and China, intercepting them at one of four phases: boost, ascent, midcourse and terminal. Interception attempts during the boost and terminal phase were virtually futile—in the former case, the window of opportunity was usually too short, and in the latter, a detonation might still destroy the target. Optimal interception, theoretically, would occur while the incoming missile was coasting through space for twenty to thirty minutes, a lag time that a launching from within America itself eliminated.

"Not a problem, sir," Roth said with perfect confidence.

"You'd stake your reputation on it?" Ridgway asked.

"I'd stake my life, sir."

"Good," Ridgway replied. "Because you've done exactly that."

Conroe, Texas

AS THE CAR rolled south toward Houston, Adlene Granger realized that she had moved beyond raw anger to another plane. Her brother's murder had inspired a quest for payback. Call it justice, but in her home state, justice frequently came from the barrel of a gun or sometimes through a needle in the arm. What it boiled down to was revenge, and who was better qualified to mete out vengeance than a Texas Ranger?

Now coming to the end of it—and maybe to the fabled End of Days itself—she found that Jerod's death had paled beside the sheer enormity of what his killers had planned for other people that she would never meet or get a chance to know. His murder left an ache inside her, and she doubted it would ever go away, but what was one man's death, even a brother's, when compared to tens of thousands?

Nothing much.

Besides, for all she knew, she had already killed his murderers. Or maybe Cooper had killed them for her. If they'd missed the men responsible, there was a good chance she'd meet them down the road, in Houston, when they crashed the madman's party at Lone Star Aerospace. And on the other hand, if they escaped, she'd likely never know it.

Did it matter?

Nowhere near as much as stopping Ridgway's crazy scheme to crown himself a king and take the country with him into ruin.

Fiddling with her smartphone, she told Cooper, "I've got like sixty rental offices in Houston, just for Enterprise. They're pretty good."

"Pick one on the west side," he instructed. "If they haven't got a van, we'll call around."

"Okay. I've got one on the Southwest Freeway. I'm calling now."

She got a clerk who sounded like he could have been in junior high school, making her feel old, but he appeared to know his business. Yes, they had a van available. A Volkswagen Crafter with a sliding cargo door on the curb side and double doors in back, plus six-speed automatic transmission, blah, blah, blah.

He quoted her a rate, and Granger put the van on hold in Matt Cooper's name. Cooper handed her a credit card for the deposit, and she rattled off the numbers, paused and listened while the sales clerk read them back.

"We're good to go," she said, when it was done.

Bolan nodded.

"You'll be the primary. Better if I don't show my driver's license, just in case."

"You're right," Cooper said. "It could be flagged, by Ridgway's people or the state."

It felt peculiar, thinking that she might now be a wanted fugitive. Were other Rangers hunting her, the old boy's network feeling their prejudgment of a female Ranger had proven accurate?

If so, she thought, to hell with them. They'd let this Ridgway business blossom right in front of them and never had an inkling that there might be something to investigate. It took her brother's death to open that Pandora's box, and even now she saw no indication that the DPS knew what was happening.

Because you haven't told them, said a small voice in her head, but Granger stifled it. Somebody should have seen this coming down the road. It wasn't her responsibility to read a crazy old man's mind, much less to save the world.

Except, today, that job *did* fall to her.

And she was praying that she wouldn't drop the ball.

Southwest Freeway, Houston

THE VAN WAS PERFECT, eight feet wide, seven feet tall, with a 2.5-liter, straight-five turbodiesel engine and could carry more than six thousand pounds of cargo, far beyond Mack Bolan's present needs. He only planned on packing in four hundred pounds or so, if that, and it would be dead weight.

The clerk Granger had talked to had their contract waiting on arrival. Bolan passed his driver's license over and signed for full insurance on the van. He didn't plan to damage it, but that was unpredictable. If nothing else, there'd be forensic clean-up charges when the vehicle came back. The company would likely sell it afterward, rather than play disclosure games with renters who might think the van was permanently soiled—or even haunted—but that wasn't Bolan's problem. He was covered on the final tab, up front, and Stony Man was picking up the Visa bill.

All that was left to do, before the madness started, was a drive-by to examine Lone Star Aerospace and spot exterior security. He couldn't plan details after that point, although he had agreed with Granger on a strategy for entering the plant. Beyond that, he would have to trust in logic, namely that the warhead Ridgway planned to launch would not be armed until the final moments before liftoff, for the sake of those involved in launching it. Arming might only take the flipping of a switch, but no one in his right mind worked around a nuke when it was primed to blow.

Of course the whole secession scheme was crazy to begin with. Could he count on Ridgway taking sane precautions now, at the eleventh hour? Maybe.

Maybe not.

It didn't matter, in the last analysis. Bolan couldn't let the rocket fly, regardless of the danger to himself and those around him when he made his final move. If there was going to be mass destruction, let it start with Lone Star's team of rocket men.

He didn't know if Ridgway would be on the premises and didn't care at this point. Heading off the launch trumped any other part of Bolan's mission. And if that turned out to be his last achievement, he knew someone else would do the mopping up.

As for the good people of Houston and its environs, if a nuke exploded in their backyard, many of them would die. One megaton, as Bolan understood it, would produce a crater two hundred feet deep and one thousand feet wide. Moving outward, no recognizable structures would survive within a radius of eleven hundred yards.

At 1.7 miles from ground zero, a few of the strongest buildings might remain standing, but 98 percent of living things exposed to the blast would be killed. Near-absolute destruction would extend another mile, though mortality would drop down to 50 percent.

At 4.7 miles, five percent of the population would die, but almost half the people in that area would be seriously injured. The damage would be moderate—with one in four people suffering wounds from flying debris—at 7.4 miles from the blast.

The bottom line: he had to hope that Ridgway wasn't quite as crazy as he seemed.

Good luck with that.

13

Lone Star Aerospace Technology

"What are we looking for again?" Jan Basson asked.

"The usual," Theo Kastner replied. "Anything suspicious." Basson grunted. "Do you reckon they can pull this off?"

"Which part?" Basson replied.

"Hell, *any* of it."

"What's the difference? I've never had a job that paid this well before. Have you?"

"Kuwait was close, but no. The trouble is, you have to live to spend it."

"Simon's got that covered. If it starts to look like it's going belly-up, we're out of here."

"Sure, I know the plan," Basson said. "Sounds good in theory. But it isn't like the damned Americans will just be sitting on their hands."

Basson himself was from South Africa. Kastner was German. Both had seen their share of mayhem under different flags, either supporting or opposing governments around the world.

"You think about that kind of thing?" asked Kastner.

"What, you don't?"

"There's no point to it," said Basson. "I never thought I'd live this long."

"That's not the same as wishing you were dead."

"Relax. I didn't sign up for a suicide. If Simon says we're ready for a bugout, I believe him."

"Guess I've just never been the trusting sort."

"You have to try it sometime," said Basson.

"Let's make it through today and see how that works out."

"Bogey at four o'clock," Basson announced, cutting the conversation short.

A white van was approaching from the west, dawdling along the curb at what amounted to a walking pace. A woman was driving, a man in the passenger's seat with a road map open before him. That role reversal struck Basson as odd enough to rate a closer look. He moved to intercept the vehicle as it slowed further, coming to a full stop thirty feet in front of him. Kastner was close behind, both men with their jackets open, granting rapid access to the MP5K submachine guns slung in fast-draw shoulder rigs.

"You want to call this in?" asked Kastner.

Basson thought about it, then said, "Better not to worry them with every little thing. Simon will think we're just a pair of *hondenaaiers*."

"Can't say that I like the sound of that."

"You shouldn't," Basson told him, smiling as he moved in closer to the van.

"So tell me what it means," said Kastner.

"When you're older. Cover me."

"You're covered."

He could see the right-hand window lowering, the man behind the street map turning toward him with a vaguely troubled look. The woman in the driver's seat—his wife, perhaps?—looked stern, as if she had been raising hell over his faulty navigation.

"Something we can do to help you?" Basson asked the map man.

"I'm afraid we might be lost," the stranger said.

"What are you looking for?"

The man mumbled something Basson didn't catch. He moved in closer to the van. "What's that you said?"

Instead of answering, the stranger raised a pistol with a silencer attached, its muzzle aimed at Basson's face from six or seven feet away. Basson had time to snarl a curse and reach for his machine pistol, before the bullet drilled his forehead, and his world went dark.

THIS WAS THE TRICKY PART—make that *one* tricky part—killing the guards and getting them inside the van unnoticed, when for all Mack Bolan knew, the whole perimeter of Lone Star Aerospace could be monitored by CCTV cameras, with reinforcements standing by for just such an emergency.

The killing was easy, a quick one-two from Bolan's liberated XD autoloader, and the sentries dropped like puppets with their strings cut. He had gone for head shots, relatively clean, although some stains were bound to mark their clothing. There was nothing he could do about it, and he'd done worse things than wearing dead men's clothes.

Shifting the bodies was more difficult, in terms of timing and exposure. They got lucky with the traffic, none approaching as he leaped out of the van and rolled back its sliding cargo door on its runners. Grabbed the nearest body and heaved it into the van by sheer brute force, turning away before the heavy *thump* of impact registered. The second corpse was heavier by fifteen pounds or so, but Bolan managed to dump it atop the first, slamming the cargo door and jumping back into his seat.

Granger was ready for him, accelerating with no flamboyant squeal of tires but making decent time. She drove two blocks, then pulled into a warehouse parking lot and cut the gas. A moment later they were both in back with two dead men, stripping the corpses of their jackets, slack and weapons.

"No peeking," Bolan warned.

"No promises."

They spent five minutes changing clothes, and while the outcome wasn't suitable for any fashion runway, Bolan thought it just might get them by. Both guards wore Lone Star name tags without photographs. He had become "J. Basson," while Granger was more or less transformed into "T. Kastner." Something less than magic, but he hoped it would do.

They left the van and walked back to the Lone Star plant, both wearing MP5K shoulder rigs and pistols they'd brought with them to the scene. They also carried long guns—Bolan's Colt, Granger's Benelli—close against their legs, and more or less concealed from any passing traffic as they strolled back to the gate that had been left unguarded in their absence.

No alarms sounded as Bolan led the way past chain-link fencing onto Ridgway's property. If they were being watched and had been spotted as impostors, he assumed there would be some reaction from the home team to contain them. Since it hadn't happened yet, the only thing to do was forge ahead.

But where to start?

Logic told Bolan they would only get one bite at the apple, and he didn't plan to waste it. The Lone Star plant and grounds sprawled over several hundred acres, more than enough space to keep them searching well past noon—if they weren't intercepted before then. Bolan's quick ground-level scan, combined with what he'd seen from satellite photos, convinced him that their best hope for discovering the rockets lay inside one of the two huge hangars standing on the north side of the plant.

And likely they would only have a chance to look at one.

"You want to split up?" Granger asked him.

Bolan thought about it while they walked. "Better not. We're pretty well outnumbered as it is."

"Okay," she said, sounding relieved. "Coin toss for hangar A or B then?"

"If we can get a look inside the first one, it should tell us what we need to know," Bolan replied. "We see a rocket getting prepped, we're in the right place."

"You'll observe that both have guards outside."

"I see them," Bolan said, knowing they likely wouldn't bluff. "They'll have to go."

"Magnificent!" said Ridgway, as he watched the semitractor couple to the gleaming rocket's transport-launcher vehicle. The tractor's fifth-wheel assembly locked into place on the first attempt, and its driver shifted from Reverse to forward motion, while a team of workmen drew the hangar's massive doors aside.

"It will be ready on your signal," Roth assured him.

"Perfect!" Ridgway checked his Rolex and beamed at everyone around him. "Eighty minutes until air time. Is the linkup ready?"

"Yes, sir," one of the technicians answered. "All we have to do is throw a switch, and you'll be live on every major network, coast to coast."

"Don't wanna drop the ball on that part," Ridgway cautioned him. "I'd hate to toast a city when nobody knows what's happening."

"You'll have a captive audience," the tech assured him.

"Awright then. Where's that little makeup gal?"

"She's waiting in the office, sir," Simon Coetzee said.

"Let's get it over with," Ridgway replied, already on the move.

He didn't like the ritual involved in getting ready for a TV broadcast, always felt peculiar with his face powdered and painted like some has-been movie star. That was one reason he'd given up on granting interviews some years ago, the other being the way those damned liberal reporters took his comments out of context to belittle him.

Smart-asses.

But he'd let them paint him up this time, because it mattered. Ridgway had a message for America and for the world. Things were about to change, and when the smoke cleared, he'd be in the driver's seat. A big frog in a small pond, maybe. But it would be *his* pond, and he was sitting on more oil than anyplace outside the Middle East.

And, hell, the way the Arabs seemed intent on killing one

another, riling up the West with threats of World War III, Ridgway just might occupy the catbird seat.

It all hung on the next few hours. First his speech, and then the shot heard round the world for real, relayed by seismographs and every television on the planet to an audience of billions.

The makeup girl who waited for him in the office was a pretty little thing, either in awe of him or doing a fair job of faking it. She blathered on about his rocket heading for the moon, the cover story she'd been fed along with everybody else, and Ridgway didn't bother contradicting her. If she got nervous, he might wind up looking like a circus clown instead of Mr. Big, the Man Who Changed the World.

Not good.

Whether he died today or lived another twenty years directing the affairs of his republic, this was no time to appear ridiculous.

He craved a double shot of Jameson and wondered if that meant he had a drinking problem. Had to smile at that, thinking it was the least of his concerns right now, as he prepared for war against the rest of the United States. An ant tackling a tiger, some might say.

But this ant had a lethal sting and was prepared to use it in just over an hour.

Surprise! he thought, and his bark of laughter spooked a squeal out of the makeup girl.

"Are you all right, sir?" she inquired.

"Don't worry, darlin'," Ridgway answered. "Me, I'm just a happy kinda guy."

BOLAN AND GRANGER were within a hundred yards of what they'd labeled hangar A when the broad doors began to roll open. They stopped to watch and saw a semitractor nose out, hauling a rocket on top of a specialized trailer. It looked small, compared to the NASA rockets that Americans had come to recognize over the years, but Bolan knew that size could be deceptive with a nuke involved.

"My God, they're really going through with it," said Granger.

"Not if we can stop them first," Bolan replied.

Bolan saw a troupe of techs and guards trailing the rocket, then scanned ahead of the slow-moving vehicle, spotting a long, low structure he had overlooked before. "Looks like a launching pad to me," he said.

The pad or platform lay about two hundred yards west of the hangar that had housed the rocket, maybe half that distance north of where Bolan and Granger stood. He counted eight shooters in the procession following the rocket, flanked by golf carts filled with workmen. At the head of the parade, two men in white lab coats rode in an open truck that Bolan took to be the rocket's launch control vehicle.

"That's Roth, in the shotgun seat," Granger said.

"All or nothing," Bolan told her. "Are you ready?"

"As I'll ever be," she answered. "Let's do it."

Bolan started jogging forward on an interception course, to meet the semitractor halfway to the launching pad. A shout, off to his right, told him the two guards left behind at hangar A had spotted them. He broke stride long enough to raise his Colt AR-15 and send two rounds down range, the hangar guards collapsing where they stood.

It went to hell from there, the way things have a tendency to do in combat. Bolan nailed the semitractor's driver with a head shot, but the rig kept rolling, despite veering off course and slowing to a crawl.

Granger was rapid-firing toward the eight guards with her twelve-gauge, running forward as she peppered them with buckshot. Bolan joined her, dropping one of them before the launch control vehicle started gaining speed, racing to catch up with the semitractor. Roth was shouting something at his driver, pointing toward the rocket on its trailer as it lost momentum.

Ridgway's men were firing back now, automatic weapons chattering, their slugs buzzing around the Executioner like angry wasps. He heard a yelp from Granger, but she kept on running, fired another blast from the Benelli, then discarded it and tore her captured MP5K submachine gun from its shoulder rig. Bolan kept firing with his carbine, spotting targets on the move, veering to intercept the launch wagon.

If someone took him down before he caught it, there was nothing to prevent the rocket being sent aloft. Nothing to stop Ridgway from taking out whatever city he'd decided to obliterate. It came down to a case of do or die, and Bolan was committed either way.

As usual.

"WHAT IN THE holy hell is that?" Ridgway demanded, bolting from the makeup chair, whipping the towel free from his neck.

The crack and rattle of gunfire, coming from somewhere outside, was clearly audible in the small office that had been transformed into a dressing room for Ridgway's televised address. The noise had spooked the makeup girl so badly she'd dropped her supplies onto the concrete floor. Ridgway was on his feet now, powder crunching under his shoes. He nearly fell when a makeup brush rolled out from under his left heel.

"Goddamn it!" he blurted, sagging until Simon Coetzee caught his elbow, holding him upright. "What *is* that?"

"I'll find out, sir." Coetzee turned as if to leave him there, but Ridgway quickly clutched *his* arm.

"Hey, not so fast!"

"Sir?"

"It's those bastards!" Ridgway said, making the only logical connection in his mind. "They've found us, and they've brung in reinforcements!"

Coetzee frowned at that. "I don't think—"

"No, you don't! *I* do the thinkin' around here. And what *I* think is that it's time for us to get the hell out."

"Sir—"

"I mean right now, goddamn it!" Ridgway bellowed.

"Of course, sir." Coetzee turned to the soldiers clustered near the office doorway. "We're leaving," he snapped. "Prep the chopper."

They had helicoptered out to Lone Star Aerospace from George Bush Intercontinental after flying from Dallas—why not, if you could afford it?—and the whirlybird was waiting for them, fifty yards from where they stood, between the hangar and the larger plant. It was an AgustaWestland AW189, with twin General Electric T700 turboshaft engines and a top speed of 173 miles per hour. Call it three minutes air time, from take-off to landing at Houston's main airport, then off in the Learjet 60 to…where, exactly?

Ridgway decided he would think about that later. Once aboard the Lear, he could fly some twenty-seven hundred miles before landing again. It was only some eight hundred miles from Houston to Mexico City, about twelve hundred to Nassau, a hair over two thousand to Maracaibo, Venezuela.

Hell, the world was his oyster.

He'd have to shift some money, pronto, before the Feds froze his Stateside accounts, but even if they'd beat him to it, there was nothing they could do about the tens of millions he had stashed in Switzerland, the Caymans, the Bahamas, and in Curaçao. Even if *all* his assets in the States were seized, Ridgway would never come up short for cash.

Provided he left *right now.*

"Let's go!" he snarled, at no one in particular, and Coetzee started shoving flunkies left and right, his soldiers joining in, clearing the Big Man's way. This was a case where money talked *and* walked, leaving the little people in its dust. What happened to the ones he left behind was their problem. Ridgway was in command, all right, but he'd be damned if he was going down with any sinking ships.

The hangar had a back door, naturally, and they exited that way, an easy jog to reach the AW189 with Coetzee and his men surrounding Ridgway, covering him with their automatic weapons. It surprised Ridgway to find that he was not frightened. The feeling he experienced was closer to excitement, tempered by the rage and disappointment of his grand scheme going up in smoke.

"We nearly did it!" he called out to Coetzee, shouting to be heard above the helicopter's whipping rotors.

"Yes, sir! Maybe next time!"

"That's a thought," Ridgway agreed.

Why not? He'd lost his grip on Texas, granted, but there was a whole wide world out there, just ripe for picking. Maybe he could find himself an island, take it off the market and declare himself a king.

Ridgway was smiling as the chopper lifted off, and humming "Dixie" to himself.

BOLAN SHOT THE driver of the launch-control vehicle, saw him slump over the wheel and heard the truck's engine begin to sputter, threatening to die. He overtook the vehicle, running like the world depended on his speed, and leaped aboard to drag the dead man from the driver's seat. George Roth, blood-spattered now, was lunging toward his own door as Bolan caught him by the collar of his lab coat, hauled him back and slammed his head into the dashboard.

Stunned, the rocket man slid halfway into the knee well on his side, while Bolan revved the clumsy vehicle and gave chase to the creeping semitractor with its lethal payload. Catching up to it, he gave his steering wheel a hard twist to the right, collided with the left-front fender of the barely moving truck, and brought it to a halt, its diesel mill still rumbling.

Rising in his open vehicle, Bolan looked back along the short course he had followed, seeking Granger. She was still there, firing short bursts from her submachine gun, taking down another one of Ridgway's shooters, while the civilian workers tried to scrambled clear.

Another glance at Roth, still moaning in his huddle, the Executioner made a move to help her out. He caught one of the Lone Star shooters circling around to Granger's left and nailed him with a 5.56 mm round from sixty feet, putting him down before he had a chance to fire.

The shot from Bolan's rifle seemed to rouse Roth from his

stupor. He struggled upright in his seat and barked, "You can't do this! It's destiny!"

"It's launch time," Bolan said, and leaned past Roth, opened his door from the inside, and shoved him from the cab, a jarring six-foot drop. Before the scientist could rise again, Bolan was at his side, hauling him erect, the AR-15's muzzle hammed beneath his chin. "What does it take to launch this bird?"

Roth gaped at him as if he were insane. "The firing stand…"

"Forget that," Bolan said, shooting a glance down range. "It's aimed already."

Roth followed his captor's gaze and blanched, seeing his rocket aimed directly at the hangar it had come from, and beyond that open building, toward the Lone Star plant itself.

"No! That's—"

Another jab from Bolan's weapon silenced him. "It's going home to roost," Bolan advised him. "You can set it up, or die and leave the job to me."

"Ignition cables," Roth gasped out. "They have to be connected."

"Do it!"

More shots crackled from the spot where he had last seen Granger, Bolan glancing back in time to see her take another Ridgway soldier down. Roth moved as if entranced, hauling a pair of heavy-duty cables from their spool at the rear of his vehicle, attaching them to the base of the forty-foot rocket. He fumbled the first try, then fixed it with Bolan's Colt pressed to the base of his skull.

"There. That's it."

"And the trigger?"

"Inside the truck's cab. The red button."

Bolan kept him covered as he backtracked to the cab and crawled inside. He couldn't miss the vehicle's command console, with its red plastic button labeled Fire. He had a finger on it as he turned back toward the Lone Star plant and saw a helicopter lifting off behind what he'd called hangar A, circling and climbing swiftly out of rifle range.

Ridgway. It had to be.

One problem at a time, thought Bolan, as he poised to press the button. "Granger!" he called back to her. "Clear out! Fire in the hole!"

She bolted from the rocket's flight path, just as Roth made one last desperate attempt to foil the launch, lunging to disconnect the cables he'd attached just seconds earlier. Bolan depressed the firing button then flung himself clear of the launch-control truck, rolling on the pavement as a searing blast of flame shot from the rocket's engine.

Roth was in the middle of it, maybe screaming, though his voice was swallowed by the roaring that drowned out all other sound. The rocket's blast melted the semitractor where it sat, together with its trailer, then the silver bird was off and speeding toward its unintended target, trailing white-hot flames. Bolan was facedown on the blacktop when it ripped through hangar A and detonated with a thunderclap that lifted him and slammed him back to earth, breathless.

The end of days, he thought. Or this day anyway.

14

College Station, Texas

Getting out was easier than Bolan had expected. The confusion helped, of course, and the successive blasts from hangar A that got its neighbor burning within minutes—rocket fuel and God-knew-what-else going up in brilliant flames—tarring the sky for miles around with thick, foul smoke. Lone Star had firefighting equipment at the plant, and sirens were converging within minutes. No one seemed to notice two bedraggled figures walking through the haze to reach their rented van or driving off to make the switch with Bolan's RAV4, half a mile away.

Bolan and Granger caught some of the action via radio, then watched the rest at a motel on State Highway 6, near the Texas World Speedway, outside College Station. Every channel had it covered, the announcers seeming awestruck with their commentary. Fox News speculated that the fire was caused by Muslim terrorists. A red-faced televangelist blamed gays and *Roe v. Wade,* then segued into praying for donations to support his ministry. Most of the talking heads were satisfied to *ooh* and *aah* over live footage of the blaze in progress. None of them, so far, had managed to obtain a comment from president and CEO of Lone Star Aerospace.

"He got away," said Granger, washing down the bitter pill with diet soda.

"In the chopper," Bolan said, confirming it.

"We've lost him then."

"Not lost. Misplaced."

"He's in the wind by now, most likely well outside the States."

Bolan had worked that out before they'd cleared the Houston city limits. He'd already talked to Brognola, who, in turn, would have relayed the news to Stony Man.

"Planes don't leave U.S. air space without filing flight plans," Bolan said. "And if they deviate, they're still on radar. Anywhere he lands, there'll be a record of it, with the plane's tail number. Same thing if he takes off for another airport."

"He could change the numbers."

"Not in flight," Bolan replied. "Whatever plane he used flying from Dallas down to Houston, it's on record. If he lands somewhere—say Mexico—and takes off overland, it still gives me a starting point."

"Gives *us* a starting point," she said, correcting him.

Bolan muted the talking heads. "You've done your part," he said, "and then some. There's no point in chasing it around the world."

"But you will?"

"That's my job. It's what I do." And who I am, he thought, but kept it to himself.

"They still owe me," she said. "For Jerod."

"If you haven't settled that tab yet, you likely never will."

"Meaning?"

"You've got a life here. A career. So far, the only people who know anything about you helping me are either dead or can't afford to talk about it. You can let it go."

"The point is that they *do* know me. Ridgway, Coetzee, whoever. What's to stop them coming back to settle up a year from now or five years on?"

"I will," the Executioner replied.

"Suppose I want to see it through. Haven't I earned that yet?"

"You've earned a break. I recommend you take it."

"No can do. You want to freeze me out, okay. I'll make believe I'm going back to work and track Ridgway myself. We'll see who gets him first."

"That's not a wise decision," Bolan said.

She smiled at that. "What have you seen me do, so far, that's *wise?*"

He watched the silent television, Lone Star going up in smoke. "Do you have a passport?"

Aboard Learjet No. N411X

FROM FORTY THOUSAND FEET, the Gulf of Mexico looked just like any other ocean on the planet. Maybe not as blue or green as parts of the Caribbean, but Ridgway wasn't interested in the scenery. Some might have said that he was running for his life, but he preferred to think of it as soaring toward a future bright with promise.

And the possibility of settling old scores.

"I want 'em," he told Simon Coetzee, who lounged in the seat beside him. "Every mother's son who had a hand in this. I don't care what it costs, how long it takes. I want their scalps."

"Figure of speech?" Coetzee inquired.

"Not necessarily."

Ridgway was not accustomed to frustration, much less to humiliation. Over the decades, since his first million had multiplied exponentially, he'd learned that problems that seemed insurmountable to lesser men were merely speed bumps on his road to ever-greater wealth and influence. Once he managed to replace the *m* in "millions" with a *b,* people stopped rejecting wild ideas and rushed to climb aboard the bandwagon.

Now some smart-ass had changed the rules, and Ridgway didn't like it. He would never rest until the insolent pissants were hunted down and punished, preferably while he watched their executions from a ringside seat.

Failing that, he'd settle for a high-def video.

In the meantime he had chosen Maracaibo as his destination of the moment. Venezuela had an extradition treaty with

the States, of course; but under President Chávez, tension between the countries had produced a breakdown in coopera-
tion on that front.

Another bonus: Venezuela currently produced more oil and
natural gas than Saudi Arabia—with domestic gasoline prices
cheaper, per gallon, than a bottle of water—and while foreign
investments were limited by law, Lone Star Petroleum had
found its niche. Ridgway had not been surprised to learn that
members of the Venezuelan government enjoyed payoffs as
much as those in Texas and Washington. The circumstances
had encouraged him to view the country as a home away from
home.

At least for now.

And in a little while… Well, who could say how long the
current president would hold on to his job? By law he could
be reelected till the end of time, but South America was well
known for its coups and revolutions. Everyone was subject to
the winds of change.

Coetzee's voice cut through Ridgway's reverie. "We'll find
them, sir. I guarantee it."

"Guarantees are one thing," Ridgway told him. "Doin' is another. I'd be lyin' if I said you haven't disappointed me so far."

"I understand, sir."

"That's a start. Now fix it!"

Turning from his window's view over the Gulf, Ridgway
stared at the television mounted in the bulkhead. He had it
tuned to CNN, and they were all over the Houston fire, with
helicopters circling through the smoke and cameras on the
ground, catching the blaze from every angle they could think
of. The networks didn't have a body count, and Ridgway wondered if they ever would, given the heat generated by rocket
fuel. A crematorium normally took a couple hours to do its
job, running at 1,400 to 1,800 degrees Fahrenheit—roughly
one-third the temperature of George Roth's modernized V-2.

Ridgway supposed it was the *late* George Roth, unless he
had been taken into custody. And there were ways to deal with

that, if it turned out to be the case. A million here, a million there…

In Ridgway's personal experience, a man could purchase anything, if he was rich enough.

A tropical sanctuary definitely. And perhaps a whole new country of his very own.

Robert F. Kennedy Department of Justice Building

"IT'S MARACAIBO," BROGNOLA said. "Landing confirmed."

Bolan's voice came back through the sat-phone. "Before I jump on that, let's wait and see if he takes off again."

"We're working on surveillance," Hal replied. "I've got a contact with the Bolivarian Intelligence Service down there. He's putting some eyes on the Learjet."

"Okay. Let's wait and see if he's refueling. If he hasn't left by sundown, say, I'll catch the next flight out. Have you got someone in the neighborhood to hook me up with hardware?"

"Shouldn't be a problem," said Brognola. "Able has a couple guys they use in Maracaibo."

Meaning Able Team—Carl Lyons, Hermann Schwarz and Rosario Blancanales, all allies of Bolan in earlier wars. Hal wasn't ready to commit them on the Ridgway problem yet, but he could field them as reserves if matters went from bad to worse.

"I'll be in touch then," Bolan said, and cut the link. No mention was made of the Texas Ranger since they'd both left Houston, leaving it to Hal's imagination for the moment.

Fair enough. The news was mostly good, so far, despite Ridgway's escape. The bulk of the mainstream media coverage leaned toward a tragic accident scenario, while state and federal authorities took command of the scene. NEST was on standby in Houston, ready to move as soon as the fires were brought under control. If and when they found fissile materials stockpiled on-site, a story could be crafted to explain them. Or the story could be buried, as others had been in the past.

Along with Ridgway, once Mack Bolan got another shot at him.

It galled Brognola that the truth about a madman's deadly power grab might never reach the public, but Hal had grown accustomed over time to unsung victories. Defeating evil was its own reward, even when victory was transient and the issue never really got resolved. He knew there'd always be another predator, another savage or a despot in the making who required the kind of treatment that the Executioner provided.

But there wouldn't always be an Executioner.

For all his skills, the one trait Bolan did not have was immortality.

THE RED PHONE on his desk trilled softly, and he grabbed it midway through the first ring.

"Yes, sir…No, that's all the information that we have right now, sir…Moving on that lead as soon as we've confirmed it, sir…You'll be apprised immediately, sir…Of course. Goodbye, sir."

Pressure from upstairs, the only person outside Stony Man who knew a thing of Hal's involvement in the covert game of life and death he played each day. There were *concerns* that had to be resolved.

What else was new?

There had been blood already, but it wasn't quite enough. Not yet.

College Station

ASIDE FROM MILITARY service, Adlene Granger hadn't seen much of the world—and what she had seen mostly left a bad taste in her mouth. Boot camp had been all right; Afghanistan had sucked. Beyond that, she had been to Mexico a few times through the years, like any other Texan, taking in the poverty of border towns like Ciudad Juárez and Matamoros, where the souvenirs—and life—were cheap.

She'd never thought about a trip to South America, much less Venezuela specifically, but it looked like she was on her way, despite Matt Cooper's initial resistance. Granger had earned her seat aboard that roller coaster, and she would ride it to the end of the line.

To Hell, if that's where it took her.

And if Hell existed, would she find her brother there?

Matt Cooper had been busy checking flights to Maracaibo, weighing charters versus the commercial airlines. They could load their weapons on a private charter plane but had no guarantee that customs would not intercept and jail them on the other end.

Conversely, if they flew unarmed on a commercial flight, Cooper believed they could find hardware when they got to Venezuela, although buying guns and ammunition in a foreign land would also be a dicey proposition. He had contacts— friends of friends, apparently—but how far could he trust them?

Granger had considered backing out, returning to her job and burying her brother as if nothing else had happened since his death. The state investigation into Jerod's murder would drag on, eventually going cold, and likely would remain officially unsolved. No one from Ridgway's camp was likely to accuse her of participating in the recent mayhem around Lone Star, but as long as the old man survived, there was a chance that someone would return to settle that account when Granger least expected it.

Choices.

Once she went aboard a flight to Maracaibo, she'd be out of options. There would be no turning back then, no second chance to face herself in the mirror—at least not with anything resembling self-respect. Whether or not she ever knew who'd pulled the trigger on her brother, whether they were dead already or had fled to parts unknown, Granger could not allow herself to go that extra mile and then beg off before the bloodletting began.

So she was in. And that meant all the way.

Cooper was on the phone again, taking another call from one of his connections. There was nothing to be gained from eavesdropping, so Granger watched the TV news, its volume turned down low. In Houston, they had more or less controlled the Lone Star fire, and folks in hazmat suits were moving in to sweep the site.

How much of what she knew for fact would ever make it to the media? Granger could not have said and was a bit surprised to find she didn't care. Reporters got it wrong so often that she barely trusted them to handle sports and weather, let alone anything that mattered. And what mattered now, to her, was finding Ridgway. Making sure he could never pull another crazy stunt like this again, regardless of how many billions he had banked offshore.

If she could help do that, it would be worth whatever risks she had to face.

And if she never made it home again…well, maybe it was worth that, too.

La Chinita International Airport, Maracaibo, Venezuela

"THEY WON'T CALL this a dry heat," Ridgway muttered, as he left the Learjet 60's air-conditioned comfort and descended into stifling humidity. It was a short walk to the limousine that waited for him on the tarmac, but he'd sweated through his shirt before he climbed inside the car and sank back in his seat.

Beside him, Malcolm Barnhart had the same sour expression on his face that he'd been wearing since Houston, seeming as if he was on the verge of tears. Ridgway considered slapping him but realized it wasn't worth the effort. He had only brought Barnhart along to keep the FBI from latching onto him and squeezing him for information. Now that they had left the States, Barnhart was moping on borrowed time.

"Is everything arranged?" Ridgway asked Coetzee.

"Good to go, sir," Simon said. "I double-checked as we were landing."

Ridgway glanced at Barnhart, who stared out the limo's tinted window to his left. "I'll need to make one stop along the way. I'll tell you when," Ridgway said.

Coetzee, as usual, raised no objections, asked no questions. He would do as he was told. Ridgway had not decided where to leave his pouting sycophant just yet, but it would come to him. Somewhere along the ninety-minute drive to his vacation *hacienda,* he would spot a place that suited him for Barnhart's execution. Burial would not be necessary. Let the Venezuelan forest deal with his disposal.

"The staff foreman was curious how long you might be staying, sir," said Coetzee.

"Was he now? I'll have to think about it."

There were legal issues to deal with, and bribes to be doled out at the so-called Ministry of Justice, to make sure that all his ducks were in a row. If something went wrong, if the bastards in charge took his money, then tried to betray him, Ridgway would have to get out on short notice.

But where would he go?

In the Western Hemisphere, only Cuba had no diplomatic ties to the United States, and Ridgway thought he was unlikely to be welcome there. Canadian law had once refused extradition of anyone facing the death penalty, but that longstanding rule was presently in legal limbo. To be clear of extradition absolutely, he would have to hide somewhere in Africa, or maybe in the Middle East.

Not an attractive prospect, either way.

Still he was hopeful Venezuela would accommodate him. Ridgway recalled reading, somewhere, that the current president received a paltry salary, less than twenty grand per year, with half of that paid out in alimony to his ex-wife. There should be some room for a negotiation there, and with the ministers who fell beneath His Excellency on the totem pole of government authority. Hell, Ridgway could keep them all in tacos and tequila for a fraction of last year's Christmas bonus out of Lone Star.

Life was good—or would be, once he verified that no G-men would be knocking on his door.

When they were fifty miles southwest of Maracaibo, outside La Villa de Rosario, Ridgway told Coetzee, "This should do it."

Coetzee nodded to the driver, and the limo coasted to a halt. Barnhart appeared to notice his surroundings for the first time since they'd landed. "What's this? Are we there?" he asked Ridgway.

"Not quite, old buddy," Ridgway said. "But this is where you leave us."

"What? I don't— What do you mean, Lamar?"

"Your services, as hoity-toity people like to say, are no longer required."

"But I don't understand!"

Barnhart apparently had not seen Coetzee exit on the far side of the limousine or walk around behind it. He let out a squawk as strong hands gripped his coat and yanked him from the car.

"Lamar! Don't do this!"

"It's already done," Ridgway replied, reaching across to close the door.

It seemed a shame to waste the limo's lovely air-conditioning.

North Terminal, Miami International Airport, Florida

BOLAN AND GRANGER opted for a commercial flight from Houston, down to Maracaibo, taking off at eight o'clock for an eleven-hour flight, with a stopover in Miami.

With more than an hour to kill in Miami, Bolan and Granger tried the Cuban fare in the surprisingly pleasant food court on Concourse D.

While they ate, they laid out basic plans for Maracaibo.

"Once we see your guy about the gear, then what?" asked Granger.

"Kill some time," Bolan replied. "We land a little after seven in the morning, and I want to make the run at Ridgway's home-away-from-home well after nightfall."

"Driving eighty miles from Maracaibo shouldn't take that long. We do the tourist thing?"

"Or just lie low. Commit the satellite photos to memory before we scout the place."

"What's the story on La Villa del Rosario?" she asked, referring to the town nearest to Ridgway's rural digs.

"It dates back to the early eighteenth century," Bolan said. "Mostly agricultural. They have about one hundred twenty thousand people spread over three parishes. The landscape that they haven't cultivated runs to jungle. Ridgway has his compound in the middle of it."

"So a night hike in the jungle. Snakes and crocodiles and jaguars. Gotta love it."

"Don't forget piranhas and electric eels."

"There'll be no skinny-dipping," Granger promised. "Are we sure Ridgway's at home?"

"He was spotted at the Maracaibo airport," Bolan said. "His people had a limo waiting."

"Even on the run, he goes in style."

"He can afford to. Two-thirds of his money lives offshore."

"And what's the status on security?"

"Nothing official," Bolan said, "according to the embassy. That doesn't mean he won't have troops on speed dial."

"Coming in from where?" asked Granger.

"It would have to be from Maracaibo."

"Giving us approximately…what? A clear half-hour on the ground?"

"About that, if they chopper in," Bolan replied. "Driving, it's closer to an hour, once they scramble."

"Split the difference, say forty minutes tops?"

"That's longer than I'd like."

"Let's hope your dealer has some special gear."

"Let's hope," Bolan agreed, and washed the last bite of his sandwich down with cold cerveza.

Until they were on the ground in Maracaibo, hoping was the best he could do.

15

Maracaibo

The contact Hal had recommended was a wiry little guy named Julio who smiled more than a normal weapons dealer should. He knew his business though and kept impressive inventory in the basement of his pawn shop, in the Barrio La Vega district. It was always risky, dealing with a total stranger in a foreign land, but Julio had dealt with Able Team and likely had a fair idea of what would happen to him if he sold out his new customers.

Bolan arrived with nothing but a wad of cash and the Honda CR-V he'd rented at the airport. It was last year's model, but he'd noted that it still looked newer than most cars on the road. He hoped the military gear on hand was better, and the dealer didn't disappoint him.

For his lead weapon, he chose a Steyr AUG, widely regarded as one of the world's most reliable assault rifles. Granger had trained on American models and went for an M4 carbine instead, both rifles chambered for 5.56 mm NATO rounds. For sidearms, they agreed on matching Beretta 92s, their muzzles threaded for suppressors that were added to the shopping list. Spare magazines and ammo, two good-size survival knives and web gear for the lot completed Bolan's list—until he spotted a Hawk MM-1 grenade launcher with a twelve-round rotating drum chambered in 40 mm. Adding ammunition for the big gun—HE, buckshot and incendiary—brought the total for his purchase to an even fifteen grand and left him satisfied.

"Ready for anything," said Granger, as they lugged their gear out to the car in OD duffel bags.

"Better to have it and not need it," Bolan said.

"Yeah, I hear you." In the SUV, she asked, "Do you figure Ridgway thinks he's ditched us?"

"If we're lucky," Bolan answered, turning back toward Via al Aeropuerto and the highway leading westward out of town. "He won't let down his guard, though."

"This will be my first time fighting in a jungle," Granger said. "The training leans toward deserts now. Some mountains. No great emphasis on hunting in the tropics."

"The terrain may differ, but it's all a jungle," Bolan said. "Concrete or sand, sirocco or monsoon. You get on with the job."

As if in answer to his observation, rain began to pelt the Honda's windshield, blowing back in streaks that seemed to flow uphill, defying gravity, as Bolan took them past the airport, where they'd landed not so long ago, and picked up speed on Highway 6, westbound toward La Villa del Rosario.

"Hey," Granger said, a few miles later, "if anything goes wrong—"

"Don't say it," Bolan interrupted her. "Bad luck."

He didn't buy that for a second, but he'd seen how negativity could work on soldiers until doubt became a self-fulfilling prophecy of failure—of death.

"Sorry," she said. "I get a little morbid sometimes."

"Leave that for the other side," Bolan advised. "We want them worried, even knowing that it doesn't help."

"How do you turn it off?" she asked.

"With lots of practice." Though, in fact, the worry gene had seemingly been left out of his makeup. He'd known fear in battle, and uncertainty, but he'd never wasted time or energy obsessing over what would happen if he lost a fight. Nobody lived forever. Understanding that before starting, making peace with it, made all the difference in the world.

Not that he planned on dying in the fight that lay ahead of him.

Like worry, he would leave that to the other side.

Rancho Refugio, Venezuela

RIDGWAY HAD NAMED his hacienda as the refuge he intended it to be, from daily life in Dallas and the world of high finance. He'd never consciously intended it to be a literal refuge or home in exile, but it came in handy, either way, now that the law would soon be snapping at his heels.

And, more than likely, someone else.

It wasn't *if* they were coming, Ridgway knew, but rather *when*. With thirty men on-site, plus living outside the city and protected by the jungle, he believed Simon could deal with troublesome intruders. An official delegation to arrest him would require some notice to the government, and even if his extradition was approved in Caracas, Ridgway had bribed enough policemen and bureaucrats to guarantee fair warning. He could be out of there before the FBI showed up to snatch him, calling it *rendition* or whatever the new label was these days.

And if they surprised him somehow, Simon had a few tricks up his sleeve, as well.

The news from Texas was still dominating U.S. television networks, but they'd backed off from a nonstop live feed to hourly updates. Ridgway saw that he had been upgraded to a "person of interest," with MSNBC first to report the discovery of nuclear materials at Lone Star Aerospace. Several newscasters were calling for a full investigation in the Senate, while a couple of the good ol' boys Ridgway had bankrolled were objecting.

None of it meant anything, now that his plan had fallen through. He had to look ahead, start thinking of tomorrow and the days beyond. Plotting his next move in the game where personal survival was his first priority, revenge a solid second.

Or he could simply let it go and use his fortune to effect a disappearance. Maybe fake his own death—how hard could it be? He'd slip into retirement with his untaxed billions, living out his golden years in quiet luxury. The hue and cry would end if Ridgway gave them a convincing corpse, and he could watch the sideshow of their inquiries as an anonymous observer, from a distance.

As for the bastards who had gone outside the rules to spoil his game in Houston, they would have to die. He'd never know a moment's peace as long as they were hunting him. Which meant that, if they failed to track him down, he'd have to hunt *them*.

Something to do. Call it a hobby, better than the canned hunts he was used to, where he paid some asshole for the chance to shoot a Bengal tiger or water buffalo on what they liked to call a "game preserve."

A real hunt was where the prey not only had a chance to live but would be shooting back.

Sipping the day's first glass of Jameson Rarest Vintage Reserve, Ridgway discovered he was actually looking forward to that hunt.

In fact he wouldn't have it any other way.

AFTER THE DRIVE from Maracaibo, and a meal in La Villa de Rosario, Bolan and Granger moved on to a scouting expedition at Ridgway's hacienda. The estate was remote enough that residents could raise hell without anyone alerting the authorities, but from the dish antennas on the roof of the main house, Bolan could tell they were in constant contact with the outside world. Not just TV and internet, but likely hot lines back to Maracaibo, maybe even Caracas.

They could summon help, but would they?

Bolan wouldn't know until the crunch came, and without that certain knowledge, he was sticking to the schedule he had planned with Granger. In and out in half an hour, give or take.

A lifetime, once the shooting started.

UNFAMILIAR AS SHE was with jungle trekking, Granger was surprised how long it took for sundown to arrive and then how suddenly night fell over the landscape. To her eyes and mind, it seemed as though the shadows lengthened slightly, then somebody hit a switch to douse the sun. Crouched next to Cooper in the midst of sounds and smells she didn't recognize, the Ranger waited for their signal to jump off.

And when it came, it nearly made her jump, regardless.

Just a simple nudge, and Cooper whispering against her ear, "It's time."

Cooper moved out first, starting the creep toward Ridgway's hacienda. Their surveillance had confirmed what satellite photography suggested: there was no fence circling the oil man's jungle hideaway. Since she knew money was not an issue, Granger guessed it had been too much trouble to install one, clearing brush and cutting trees along the way. The forest formed a wall of sorts around Ridgway's remote estate, but Cooper seemed to have no trouble penetrating it.

She followed him as closely as she could, given the darkness underneath those looming trees that blocked out moonlight from above. Compared to Cooper, Granger felt like an ungainly amateur, convinced she must be making noise enough to wake the dead as they advanced. He didn't turn to shush her though, which helped a little with her flagging confidence.

Her M4 carbine was a tricked-out model, with a vertical fore grip, an Aimpoint CompM3 red-dot sight and a hundred-round ammo drum to get her started. If she needed more than that once battle had been joined, she had a dozen thirty-rounders in a bandolier across her chest. It felt like overkill, but there was Cooper with the MM-1, besides his Steyr AUG, so who was she to say?

And after the firefight and what followed back at Lone Star Aerospace, she realized it was better to have too much hardware than to come up short and die as a result.

You could die anyway, a nagging voice in her head reminded her, but she ignored it. She had a job to finish here. The fact that no one had assigned her to it, and she wasn't getting paid a penny for her time, made no damn difference at all.

This was for Jerod and for her. To stop Ridgway's insanity from ever raising up its ugly head again.

RIDGWAY COULD SMELL carnitas cooking in the kitchen, Rosalita whipping up a feast fit for a king. It pissed him off to think he could have been a president by now, but what would be the fun of gambling if he knew each hand of cards was guaranteed to be a winner?

Sipping whiskey while he waited for supper, Ridgway thought he knew where he'd gone wrong. Trusting a German with the rocketry, for starters, even knowing that he was a third-generation goose stepper at heart. A damned crackpot, no matter how good he might be on the tech side. Then there'd been Walraven, fired by the NNSA for some kind of malfeasance. Who knew where he might have told tales out of school or to whom?

Things to consider before next—

The house shook suddenly, as if someone had dropped a boulder on the roof. The mighty *thump* of an explosion startled Ridgway, made him bolt out of his easy chair and drop his half-full whiskey glass. He made a beeline for the exit from his study, but before he reached the door a second blast sent tremors rippling through his tropical dream house, pale dust falling from the ceiling overhead.

"Not yet!" he said to no one in the empty den. Diverting from the exit, Ridgway opened up a built-in cabinet and grabbed a vintage Colt M1911 autoloader from its hook, checking the pistol's load before he tucked it under his belt. He backed that up with a Remington Model 870 pump-action shotgun, its extended magazine loaded with eight rounds of double-O buck.

Maybe his eyes weren't great, but with the twelve-gauge, he could still drop anything that he could see within, say, thirty yards. He'd let his soldiers do the brunt of the fighting obviously, but if anyone got past them, Ridgway would be ready for the no-good bastards.

They could face the big dog then, and see what happened.

But he was *frightened* now, goddamn it, which he found infuriating for a man of his age and accomplishments, the fortune he'd accumulated from his own hard work and that of others. Who were these pissants to make him cringe and tremble?

No, by God! If this was meant to be his final day on earth, the least that he could do was stand up to his enemies and take it like a man. Teach them that they were in a fight with someone who had never quit or cut and run away.

Well…not unless you counted running out of Houston with his tail between his legs.

Snarling, he jacked a round into the shotgun's chamber, started for the door again—

And was immediately toppled to all fours by yet another blast shaking his house. This one seemed to be right on top of Ridgway, raining plaster dust all over him. Outside he heard the Spanish barrel tiles cascading from his roof and shattering on impact with the patio. The place was coming down around him, and the only thing he could think of now was getting out.

Before it was too late.

BOLAN FIRED ANOTHER round from the Hawk MM-1, the HE penetrating a kitchen window on the south side of the ranch house, where it detonated with a crack of smoky thunder. Almost instantly a secondary blast sent bright flames leaping up the walls inside, probably a propane tank that fueled the stove. Before he passed the shattered window, smoke was pouring out of it and he heard men shouting in the house, English and Spanish mixing as they prepared to fight the fire.

Good luck with that.

He moved on, Granger covering his back with short bursts from her M4 carbine. Floodlights had already blazed to life, turning the hacienda's grounds as bright as noon, but Bolan had his next attack spotted. He lined up the round from his 40 mm launcher. When it struck the shed that housed the generator, sparks flew, then the gasoline reserve went up in flames. Suddenly the property went midnight-dark again.

Night favored the intruders, although some of Ridgway's men had flashlights mounted on their automatic weapons, pale beams lancing through the darkness, seeking targets. Bolan dodged them, switching to his Steyr AUG and firing three-round bursts at shadow-figures flitting here and there across his path. In the confusion, he was able to proceed another thirty yards before he started drawing hostile fire, but even then most of the hasty shots went high and wide.

It seemed to Bolan that a few of Ridgway's men, at least, were running now, instead of settling in to fight. Seeing the house in flames had evidently changed some minds about the wisdom of continuing a battle in the dark with unknown enemies. Bolan guessed that most of those retreating were the local help, and that was fine. Each shooter who bugged out was one less Bolan had to kill, one less who might get lucky killing him.

Behind him, unexpectedly, a cry of pain from Granger came together with the echo of a pistol shot. Bolan turned back to look for her and found her on the ground, a man kneeling beside her with an autoloader pressed against her head. Firelight on half his face identified the new arrival on the scene as Simon Coetzee, Ridgway's security chief.

"We've been a long time getting here," the South African said.

"You should have stuck around in Houston," Bolan replied.

"The boss thought otherwise. You know how that goes."

"Running didn't help him."

"No. But now you're done."

"Think so?"

"I've read about this one," said Coetzee, leaning on the pistol until Granger gasped. "A little lady playing soldier. Should've pissed off when I killed the brother, shouldn't she? Now look at her. After tonight, there'll be no Grangers left at all."

"And one less Coetzee," Bolan answered, sighting down the barrel of his auto rifle.

"Maybe. Thing is, I believe I'm fast enough for both of you."

"Prove it."

Coetzee smiled at him and never saw it coming, Granger whipping out the knife she'd picked in Maracaibo, reaching up and back to drive its nine-inch blade into his thigh. He bellowed, tottered backward, might have killed her even then, but Bolan's three-round burst of 5.56 mm manglers ripped through Coetzee's face and sheared off half his skull before the signal from his brain could reach his trigger finger.

Granger rolled away from him, came up on hands and knees, clutching her side as Bolan reached her. "I'm all right," she said. "Get after Ridgway. Finish this!"

He took the lady at her word and left her, once she'd risen to her feet and proven she could stay there, with the M4 in her hands. Around her, Ridgway's men were either down or on the run.

Bolan moved on into the smoky darkness. Hunting.

LURCHING FROM THE ruin of his ranch house, Ridgway dropped his plan for battling the unseen enemy and staggered toward the line of vehicles that stood some fifty yards to the north. He wanted out, away from there, and wasn't waiting to collect a driver or a team of bodyguards. From what he saw and heard around him, it appeared that many of his men had already deserted him, the lily-livered cowards.

Simon would be somewhere in the midst of it, no doubt, but that was too damned bad. He was a soldier, drawing hazard pay, and now he had a chance to earn it or die trying. Ridgway liked him well enough, but, hell, it wasn't like the two of them were family. Coetzee was just another hireling who had let him down.

Screw him.

The first car Ridgway came to was a Ford Explorer. Keys in the ignition naturally, so the boss could take a spin around the hacienda anytime he wanted to—or in a pinch, like now, run for his life. Ridgway slid in behind the wheel and propped his Remington across the empty seat beside him, easily within his reach. He turned the key and revved the 4.0-liter V-6, feeling its power through his hands and feet.

A few more minutes and he'd be away from there, hightailing back to Maracaibo where the Learjet 60 waited for him, fueled and ready for a hop to somewhere else, another hideout where he'd finally be safe.

Ridgway switched on the headlights, gasping at the vision of a tall man dressed in camouflage fatigues, standing some thirty feet in front of him, holding a weapon that resembled an inflated version of an old-time tommy gun. Its stovepipe muzzle seemed to be aimed straight at Ridgway's face.

"All right, you pissant!" Ridgway muttered. "Show me what you've got!"

He stamped on the accelerator, hurtling forward, as the stranger fired into the Ford Explorer's grill. Ridgway could actually *see* the fat projectile flying toward him, then it struck, and he was in a spinning hell of fire, smoke, thunder, as the SUV stood on its nose, then slowly toppled over on its roof.

MACK BOLAN CROUCHED beside the Ford and peered in through the shattered driver's window. Ridgway lay contorted on the vehicle's inverted ceiling, legs twisted, his face a mask of blood. One eye focused on Bolan as he wheezed, "Who are you?"

"Just a soldier," Bolan answered.

"Bull…shit. Tell me, damn it."

"What's the difference?"

Above him, on the capsized undercarriage of the SUV, a burst of flame erupted, then began to spread along the fuel line.

"Have to…know," Ridgway insisted.

"I've always thought the trouble with this part was too much talk."

Bolan silenced Ridgway with a point-blank 5.56 mm mercy round and went to look for Granger in the night.

Epilogue

Miami International Airport

"The doc in Maracaibo wasn't bad," Granger said. "I definitely like those pills he gave me."

"They use good people at the consulate," Bolan agreed.

"I thought they'd ask more questions. Well, *some* questions, anyway."

Instead of getting into Hal and how he'd pulled some strings, Bolan replied, "They didn't want to know."

"Makes sense, I guess. Am I allowed to ask you where you're going next?"

"I won't know till I get there," Bolan said. A small lie, better for them both.

"Ships passing in a stormy night, I guess."

"It happens."

They were calling Granger's flight now. She rose from her seat with the barest hint of a wince. "Well, if you're ever back in Texas…"

"Right."

"Who am I kidding, eh?"

She kissed him on the cheek and turned away, proceeding to her boarding gate without a backward glance. Bolan stood watching, to be sure, then shrugged it off and moved along the concourse toward his own gate. Still another forty minutes left to kill before the flight he'd booked to Richmond and a rental ride to Stony Man.

He might be back in Texas someday, but they both knew that he wouldn't call, wouldn't disrupt the Ranger's life once it had settled back to normal. If it could.

His normal was the hell grounds, and another battle waited for him, maybe coming up tomorrow or the next day after that.

The Executioner was moving on.

* * * * *